The Last of the Good Guys

The Last of the Good Guys

Ernesto Patino

First published by L&L Dreamspell in 2011

Cover design by Eric Durr

This is a work of fiction, and is produced from the author's imagination. People, places and things mentioned in the novel are used in a fictional manner.

ISBN-10: 0692825673
ISBN-13: 9780692825679
Published by Lazy Lizard Press
Printed in the United States of America

For Diana

CHAPTER 1

South Florida

"Will you be okay?" Alec Santana said to Julie Brody after the last of the mourners had left.

She had to think about it. "I don't know because I don't know what I'm supposed to feel. I mean, if only he had left a letter, a note, anything…" Her lips quivered. "There were never any secrets between us. That's why none of this makes any sense."

He reached for a half-empty bottle of wine, poured a little into a glass and handed it to her. "You look as though you could use it." He poured himself a glass and sat beside her.

"What about the police? Did they come up with anything?"

She sighed. "They had a body, a gun and the medical examiner's opinion that Ben had shot himself. To them, it was just another suicide. End of case."

"Well, suicide or not, Ben must have had a reason. Was he acting strangely or was he upset about something in particular?"

She started to shake her head. "As a matter of fact, there *was* something—right after he opened a letter he got nine or ten days ago. He said it was a bill he'd forgotten to pay and I really had no reason to disbelieve him. The next day he seemed just fine. But then a couple of days later, he woke in the middle of the night, trembling and breathing rapidly, as though he'd just broken free from a nightmare. He had always slept like a log, so I knew something was bothering him, but I never imagined it was anything serious."

"Did he ever show you the letter?"

"No. And when I asked him about it a few days later, he acted like he didn't know what I was talking about. I shrugged it off and basically put it out of my mind. The clues were there, but I didn't put them together." She reached to pick up a small photograph of Ben holding up a small shark he'd caught on the Gulf side of Marathon Key. She stared at it for a moment, and then reached to wipe a tear from the corner of her eye.

"I'm sorry, I'm upsetting you and you probably want to be alone."

"No, no." She put down the photograph. "Actually I'm glad you're here because maybe…well, you being his friend, I thought you might have some ideas of your own. Sometimes friends say things to each other that they wouldn't necessarily want to share with their wives."

Alec took a sip of his wine. "I really can't think of a single thing he said or did that would explain what was troubling him. The last time I saw him was about two weeks ago. We played a round of golf and he seemed his usual self. In fact, he kept talking about a Caribbean cruise that he'd been planning for the past few days."

"A cruise? That's odd; he never mentioned one."

"I think he wanted to surprise you. Anyway, that's all I can remember, which isn't much help, I'm afraid."

Julie drew a long deep breath. "I'll tell you one thing. I'll never have any peace until I know what really happened. Something drove him over the edge. One way or another I've got to find out what it was."

"How are you going to do that? You said yourself that the police had closed the case, which means—"

Julie half-smiled. "Which means that someone who used to be a pretty good cop could easily pick up where they left off."

Alec shook his head. "I'm an Insurance Claims adjuster for God's sake. Besides, what's it going to prove? And if or when you discover the truth, it won't bring him back."

"Look, Alec, I know you don't understand and I really can't blame you. But will you please think about it?"

"You know of course, that the truth may turn out to be something… well, something you'd be better off not knowing."

"I'm prepared to accept it," she said, pursing her lips.

"Well, if it means that much to you." He rose. "But do me a favor. Why don't you sleep on it, or better yet, give it a few days? If you still feel the same way…"

Julie forced a smile as she walked him to the door. "Thanks for being such a good friend, to both of us." She kissed him on the cheek and closed the door.

Alec tried not to act surprised when she called the next morning. "You're really serious about this, aren't you? I hoped you'd let it rest, at least until you've had a chance to put it into perspective."

"Sounds like you're having second thoughts. Not that I blame you."

"Look, I know how much this must mean to you, but—"

"You don't have to explain. It was unfair of me to even suggest it. It's my problem and I'll deal with it the best I can. Maybe I'll hire a private investigator. You wouldn't happen to know of one, would you?"

A long silence, and then a sigh. "I've got a lot of vacation leave built up and I was thinking that maybe now would be a good time to take some days off. Ben was my friend. I owe it to him to find out what made him do it."

"Thank you," she said softly. "You don't know how much this means to me. Where will you begin?"

"I'm not sure. Maybe I'll talk to the detective who handled the case. He could be holding back on something. It's hard to explain but cops sometimes know more than they want to share with the public, especially a man's wife."

"I don't understand. Why would they keep important details from me?"

"I'm not saying they are. I'm only saying that, well, let me give you an example. Suppose a guy is found dead, say from a heart attack, in some sleazy motel. And suppose someone reports seeing a cheap hooker leaving his room. In a case like this the cops may or may not tell the guy's wife about the hooker. What would be the point? They'd write it up as just another heart attack victim, plain and simple. What I'm trying to say is that you never know what you'll find until you start asking questions."

She paused for a moment. "I want you to know that I really appreciate you taking the trouble to do this for me. I loved Ben so much and if I don't…"

"I understand." He nodded. "Just give me a few days, okay?"

"You're a good friend, Alec. If there's any way I can help, let me know. One last thing. I-I hope you won't keep the truth from me, especially if it turns out to be something unpleasant. Promise you won't hold anything back."

He hesitated. "I promise. Good, bad or whatever, you'll be the first to know."

CHAPTER 2

From across his desk, Detective Palafox looked at Alec and shook his head. "That's about it. It was an open and shut case. The guy's prints were all over the gun. I mean, does it really matter why he offed himself? People kill themselves every day. Some leave notes, some don't."

Palafox's partner, Detective Riley, nodded in agreement but didn't say anything.

"What about the crime scene? Did you find anything, anything at all?" Alec asked.

"Crime scene?" Detective Palafox said. "You've been watching too many cop shows. Look, the guy sticks a gun in his mouth and pulls the trigger. What was there to investigate? The medical examiner ruled it a suicide and that was good enough for us."

Alec rubbed the back of his neck and stood up. "I guess that's it, then. I was hoping you might have found something that… Well, never mind. I've got my work cut out for me, that's for sure. Thanks." He started to walk away.

"Wait a second," Detective Riley said. "I just remembered something. It's probably nothing, but right after we found him, a call came in from a woman who didn't give her name. Anyway, she asked if a letter was found near the body."

"What letter?"

"That's what I asked. Then she hung up. I thought it was a little strange, but afterward, I just shrugged if off. Probably some creep with a morbid curiosity."

Alec frowned. "Thanks. Thanks a lot."

After leaving Detective Palafox's office, Alec couldn't get Detective Riley's comments about the letter out of his mind. He wondered if Ben was in the middle of something, perhaps a business deal that went terribly wrong. He drove over to Greynolds Park where Ben's body had been found slumped in his car. He saw nothing unusual. When he spotted several torn, crumpled pieces of paper caught underneath a large bougainvillea bush a few feet away, he walked over and gingerly retrieved them. They appeared to be from a machine printed note or a letter. A heavy rainfall had soaked them and the print was blurred, except for some words here and there that didn't make any sense. After a moment, he slipped the papers in his pocket. Then he got back in his car and left the park.

When Julie answered the door, she looked pleasantly surprised. "You found something already?"

Alec followed her to the living room. "I did, but I'm not sure what to make of it." He showed the pieces of paper to her. "I found these under a bush near where Ben's car was parked. I talked to the detectives who handled Ben's case. One mentioned that a woman had called to ask if a letter had been found near Ben's body."

"Who was she?"

"She didn't identify herself. When the detective denied knowing anything about any letter she hung up."

Julie became quiet for a moment. "You don't suppose Ben was—"

"Having an affair? No way. Ben was a straight arrow. He loved you too much to ever cheat on you. Besides, if he were seeing someone else, I think I would have known about it."

"So if Ben didn't know her, why did she call?"

He shrugged. "Maybe it's someone you both knew. Didn't you mention something about a letter Ben received?"

"You think the woman was talking about the same letter?"

"I don't know, but I intend to find out." He stood up. "I've got a friend who works at the county crime lab. I'm going to show him these scraps and see what he can make of them. I'll call you if it turns out to be something interesting. But don't build your hopes up too much. It could turn out to be some kid's English assignment." He chuckled.

CHAPTER 3

The phone rang as Alec entered his apartment.

"Turn on Channel 7," Julie said. "I'll explain later."

With his other hand Alec picked up the remote and pressed the On key.

"We're in front of a house where less than four hours ago, a man named Stuart Mendoza was found hanging from a beam in the garage," said the reporter, a young woman with a shrill voice and a rapid delivery. "He lived here along with his wife, Martha and their teenage daughter. According to a police spokesperson, Mr. Mendoza left a note, which they speculate might be a suicide note. He reportedly had been despondent for several days. The medical examiner and homicide detectives are still in the house finishing up their investigation."

From the corner of her eye, the reporter spotted the man's wife coming out of the house. She ran toward her and shoved the microphone in her face. "Mrs. Mendoza, can you please tell us why you think your husband took his own life? Was he depressed about something? How is your daughter taking it?"

"It's a family matter. Please leave us alone." She and her daughter rushed to a waiting car.

The reporter then turned to a neighbor, a gray-haired, unshaven man standing next to a white pickup. "Did you know Mr. Mendoza well?" She held the microphone up to him.

"Oh sure. I've lived next door to him for over twenty years. It's just awful. He was a kind, decent man. Used to be a police officer, you know, and a darn good one."

"Can you think of any reason why he would take his own life?"

The neighbor shook his head. "He always seemed to be in good spirits. But I guess like all of us, there are things you keep to yourself."

Alec turned off the TV. "Poor guy," he said into the mouthpiece. "He left the force a year or two after I did. I never figured him as the type who would kill himself, though. But then I didn't think Ben would either."

"Listen, this may sound crazy, but what are the odds of two ex-cops from the same police department committing suicide within days of each other?"

"You think there's a connection?"

"I don't know. Maybe I'm just grasping at straws. At this point, I'm willing to believe almost anything that sounds even remotely possible."

"I just thought of something," Alec said after a pause. "Mendoza was one of the cops who saved a little boy from a burning fire just before Christmas…fourteen, fifteen years ago. Come to think of it, Ben was there too. There were others but I can't remember their names."

"Ben had been on the force only a couple of years. We had just moved into our current house."

Alec scratched his chin. "I think I'll pay Mendoza's widow a visit. But I'll wait 'til after the funeral."

"What do you think she can tell you?"

"I'm not sure. But we have nothing to lose."

CHAPTER 4

"So what do you think?" Alec asked from across the documents examiner's desk.

Cecil Silverman adjusted his jeweler's magnifying glass and moved the pieces of paper closer to the light from a Halogen lamp. "I don't know, the water damage is extensive. I hope you're not in a hurry. Why don't you leave it with me and give me some time to work on it. I can't promise anything, but you'll at least have more letters, maybe more words."

"That's all I wanted to know. Just give me a call when you finish. I owe you one."

"I'm glad you said that." A smile formed across Cecil's round, ruddy face. "Remember I told you about my wife's cousin from Pittsburgh, the one that just got divorced? Well, she's coming to town next week. My wife thought maybe the four of us could—"

Alec started to back away. "Oh, no. I'm not falling for that one again. Last time it was her old college roommate. You know how I feel about blind dates."

"It would really mean a lot to me, and it would get my wife off my back. I'll even pick up the tab. So what do you say?"

Alec smiled. The guy was doing him a favor, after all. The least he could do was help him out this time, this *one last time*. "All right, but I get to pick the place."

A week later Alec drove over to Stuart Mendoza's house in West Fort Lauderdale. He had met his wife once or twice when he was still with the department. He hoped she'd remember him.

"Alec Santana," Mrs. Mendoza repeated. She kept her hand on the partially opened door. "I'm sorry, but I don't remember you."

"Well, it was a long time ago. I left the department before Stuart." He cleared his throat. "I know this may not be the right time, but I wonder if I can talk to you for a few minutes. May I come in?"

Mrs. Mendoza hesitated a second, and then opened the door wider. "I guess it's all right. Please come in." She led the way to the living room, which had the faint smell of burning candles. There were two of them, on either side of a small picture of Stuart in police uniform. The portrait sat on top of a mantel, along with a set of black Rosary beads and a small, propped up picture of the Sacred Heart of Jesus.

They took a seat across from each other.

"Stuart missed being a policeman." She stared at his photograph. "That was his favorite picture." She sniffled and wiped her teary eyes with her hand. "I'm sorry. It's so hard for me to believe he's really gone."

"I understand." He gave her a moment. "Does the name Ben Brody sound familiar?"

She shook her head. "I'm not very good with names. Was he one of Stuart's friends?"

"I'm not really sure. He used to be a police officer and he happened to be my friend. He killed himself a few days ago and his wife thought that—"

Her eyes widened. "He committed suicide?"

"It looks that way. His wife, her name is Julie, can't understand why he did it. One moment he was fine and the next, he decides to end it all by shooting himself." He paused. "She's asked me to look into it. That's why I'm here, to see if maybe Stuart and Ben had something in common."

"Besides both being former policemen?"

Alec nodded. "Unfortunately Ben didn't leave a suicide note so we don't have much to go on." He hesitated. "I know this is very painful for you but did you keep a copy of Stuart's note?"

"I can show it to you." She went to the den and returned with a copy of the note and an old newspaper clipping.

"I told the detectives I wanted a copy of it." She handed it to him. "They still have the original."

Alec scanned the note:

Dear Martha,

I wish I could explain what this is all about, but I can't. Someday the truth will come out, and when it does, I hope it won't change the way you feel about me. I agonized over it for days, and saw no other way. Please forgive me.
Your loving husband,
Stuart

"Was Stuart in some kind of trouble?" He set down the note and stared at Mrs. Mendoza.

She hesitated. "It's rather personal. Not that it matters anymore. When the police asked me about the note, I said I didn't know what Stuart was referring to. But that's not entirely true. I was too embarrassed. The truth is, I think Stuart was having an affair. He's had many during our marriage and a few of them got pretty ugly. The worst was when he fathered a baby with a woman who worked at the dry cleaners. That was ten years ago."

"You think that's what the note was about? About some affair that went wrong?"

She shrugged. "When I first read it, that's the first thing that went through my mind." She glanced at the newspaper clipping in her hand, and then handed it to him. "I don't know if this means anything, but I found it inside one of his jackets. I hadn't seen it in years."

"This is the article about the boy Stuart saved from the fire." Alec looked at the picture of Stuart kneeling over the young boy he had just rescued. In the background were four other officers: Ben Brody, Roy Harrison, Jeff Conway, and Rudy Johnson. He read the article:

HERO OFFICER SAVES LIFE OF YOUNG BOY

Police officer Stuart Mendoza is already being called a hero. At about 11:45 p.m. Christmas Eve he rushed into a burning house to rescue an eleven-year-old boy who was trapped inside. It is believed the blaze that killed the boy's parents started when a string of lights short-circuited and ignited the family Christmas tree.

According to a police spokesperson, Officer Mendoza and his partner Roy Harrison had been on routine patrol just a few blocks away when they spotted the flames and rushed to the scene. Minutes later they were joined by officers Rudy Johnson, Jeff Conway and Ben Brody, all of whom tried unsuccessfully to go back into the burning house to rescue the boy's parents. By the time firefighters arrived, the fire was out of control and there was no hope of finding anyone else alive.

Alec studied the picture again. "Did Stuart maintain contact with the other police officers, Harrison, Johnson and Conway? You already said Ben's name wasn't familiar to you."

"If he did, he certainly didn't tell me about it. Now that I think about it, after that night Stuart hardly ever talked about the incident. A couple of times when I brought it up he changed the subject, so I never mentioned it again."

"May I keep these?" Alec held up the note and the article.

"You can have them," she said, after a brief hesitation. "All I ask is that you let me know if you uncover something about Stuart and the reason he killed himself."

He nodded. "I will."

They stood up simultaneously.

"I...don't know how to say this." She fought to hold back the tears. "I mean, I know you must wonder why I stayed with Stuart after so many of his affairs."

"You don't owe me an explanation."

"But I want to," she insisted. "Now that he's gone, somebody should know the truth. In a way it's easier to tell a stranger." She looked away and then back at him.

"You see, when I first met Stuart he was every woman's dream: handsome, well-mannered and oh, so charming. I was basically a plain Jane and couldn't compete with all the girls who always seemed to be around him. To make a long story short, Stuart eventually asked me out and a few months later we were married. He could have had any girl he wanted, but he chose me and—I know how this must sound—it made me feel grateful. Even when he was having his affairs he could have walked out of my life, but he never did. So maybe he wasn't the best husband or maybe I just never stopped feeling grateful. Anyway, I just wanted you to know."

"He was a lucky man, your husband." Alec didn't know what else to say as he stood there for a moment and then quietly turned to leave. "I'll be in touch."

CHAPTER 5

Julie read the note and then the article. "I don't understand," she said from across her kitchen table. "What does this have to do with Ben's suicide?"

Alec looked at her. "I was hoping you might have an answer. Did Ben ever talk about these guys, any of them?"

She shook her head. "They weren't his close friends, that's for sure. I vaguely remember a couple of the names, Rudy Johnson and Roy Harrison. But that was when Ben was still on the force."

"Stuart's widow didn't remember them at all. Didn't even know if Stuart had maintained contact with any of them."

"So what next?"

"Well, I'd like to talk to the others, the ones mentioned in the article. I know Roy Harrison died of lung cancer about eight years ago and both Conway and Johnson had resigned, which means I'll first have to find them."

"You really think there could be a connection?"

Alec shrugged. "I don't know, but it's worth checking out. In the meantime why don't you go through Ben's papers and stuff and see if you come up with anything that might show a tie-in." He glanced at his watch. "I've got to get going. Don't want to be late for my blind date."

"Blind date? Now I've heard everything. I didn't realize you were that desperate." She stifled a laugh.

"Laugh all you want but this is the price I have to pay to have someone analyze the papers I found in the park. The county document examiner is an old friend of mine. He and his wife suggested we make it a foursome—my date being her cousin from Pittsburgh. I tried to say no but, oh well, maybe it won't be so bad."

"You can handle it. You might even enjoy yourself."

"If I do, it'll be a first." He grinned. "Blind dates are not my idea of a good time." He got up and started for the door. "Any chance you could beep me, say around 8:30 p.m.? You could be my emergency excuse to bug out of there."

She laughed and shook her head.

"Didn't think so. I'll let you know how it went."

The next day, Alec called an old buddy and got current addresses for Jeff Conway and Rudy Johnson. Conway lived in Fort Lauderdale, Johnson in Homestead. He'd try Conway first since he was closest.

Conway owned a house in the new part of Coral Ridge, a pricey, semi-yuppyish neighborhood on the west side of the Intracoastal Waterway. He had married well, which explained why he could afford to live there and why he'd left the force after only a few years.

Alec rang the bell, waited a couple of seconds, and then rang it again. No answer. He started to walk away when someone opened the door.

"Yes, can I help you?" said a tallish, slender woman with an oval face and a pale, silky smooth complexion. She wore a white, paint-splattered smock that smelled of mineral spirits.

"I'm sorry, I thought no one was home. I'm looking for Jeff Conway."

"You obviously don't know," she said, her voice somber. "My husband passed away two weeks ago. May I ask why you're looking for him?"

"I don't know what to say. I had no idea; please forgive me. My name is Alec Santana. Jeff and I used to be on the force many years ago. Do you mind if I ask how he died? Was he ill?"

"He committed suicide. You still haven't said why you wanted to see him."

"May I come in? I'll explain everything."

She hesitated. "Well, only for a moment. I'm in the middle of a painting." She led the way to her studio toward the rear of the house. "If you don't mind, we can talk while I work." She picked up her brush. "I've got to meet a deadline for an exhibition next week."

"Interesting." Alec looked at the large unfinished canvas, a surrealistic painting of a nude couple, a man and a woman, surrounded by angels sitting on white billowy clouds. In the background—the symbolic gates of heaven with a small sign that said NO VACANCY.

"So what is it you want to talk about, Mr. Santana?" She dabbed her brush with white paint and used fine strokes to work around the edge of the clouds, which looked like large cotton balls.

"Do the names Ben Brody and Stuart Mendoza mean anything to you?"

She shook her head. "Are they supposed to?"

"They were ex-cops on the force around the same time your husband was there. Both of them recently committed suicide."

Mrs. Conway stopped what she was doing. "Now I'm really curious. What *exactly* is your interest in all of this?"

"Ben Brody was my friend. His wife asked me to look into his death. Julie took it pretty hard because he left no note, nothing to indicate what made him do it. It doesn't make any sense. They had a pretty good marriage and no big problems to speak of."

Mrs. Conway put down her brush and walked over to small rattan couch. "Tell me more." She sat down.

Alec took a seat across from her. "Let me show you something." He handed her the article Mrs. Mendoza had given him.

Mrs. Conway took her time reading it. "I had forgotten all about it." She handed back the article. "You think the deaths are related, somehow?"

"That's what I'm trying to figure out. If it's not too personal, can you tell me how Jeff killed himself?"

"The day it happened, he called me from some pay phone. He said he hoped I'd understand, that he was doing it for me. He didn't make any sense. He started to cry and I could hardly understand him and then he hung up. Unfortunately I didn't take his call as seriously as I should have. If I had, I might have gone out and looked for him, maybe talked him out of it." She shook her head. "The next day, the cops showed up at my door and told me Jeff's car had been found near a bridge in Boynton Beach. The keys were in the ignition and his wallet was left on the seat of the car. They said some fisherman had spotted him standing by the side of the bridge about midnight."

"What about his body?"

"It was never found. A couple of days later, I received a letter from Jeff. He had mailed it the day he killed himself. He said he loved me and that he was doing it to protect me. He gave no explanation."

"Did you show the letter to the police?"

"I burned it. I know it was a stupid thing to do, but I didn't want the cops or the press to make a big deal out of it, like they usually do. I did tell the cops about it and of course, they immediately thought I was hiding something, which I wasn't."

Alec rubbed his chin. "Did Jeff ever mention the cops in the article? Did he have any contact with them that you know of?"

"To be honest, I never paid much attention to his friends. For all I know they may have been his drinking buddies." She paused. "Look, you may as well know the truth. My husband and I didn't have a good marriage. We had what you might call, an arrangement. He married me for my money and I married him because…well, it's really not important. The truth is, I had already decided to divorce him."

Alec waited a moment, and then stood up. "Well, I know you have to finish your painting, so I'll be on my way. Thanks for hearing me out." He motioned for her to remain seated. "I'll see my way out."

Mrs. Conway got up and walked back to her painting. "By the way," she said from across the room, "my show is next Wednesday night at the Cantrell Gallery on Las Olas Boulevard. If you happen to be in the neighborhood…" She flashed a soft smile that lingered a couple of seconds.

Alec turned and looked at her. "Thanks, I might just be there."

Later as he entered the expressway, he got a call from his friend Cecil. He'd finished examining the water-stained papers. "Sorry it took so long. You can stop by whenever you want and I'll show you what I was able to do."

"I'll be right there." Alec dropped the phone on the passenger seat.

Alec studied the papers and a work sheet that Cecil had used to compose probable word combinations. "None of this makes any sense. There are still too many missing words."

"It's the best I could do. The rain had pretty much wiped out most of the ink that came from an inkjet printer. If you want I can work on it some more, maybe try a few other things."

"That's all right. I know you did your best."

Cecil thought about it for a second. "Look, if this is really important to you there's something else we can try. There's a state-of-the-art lab in Atlanta that has a lot more stuff than we do. They're pretty busy though, and they may take longer than you're willing to wait."

Alec looked at him, nodding. "Let's do it. When can you send it out?"

"First thing in the morning."

"Thanks, I owe you, again." He smiled, then added, "And the answer is no in case you're thinking of trying to fix me up with another one of your wife's cousins."

"I wasn't going to say anything." Cecil raised his hands. "Anyway, my wife's giving up on you. You've been a bachelor too long. She thinks you're too serious, too set in your ways."

Alec chuckled. "Maybe she's right. Just don't spread it around."

CHAPTER 6

Across rows of uneven monuments Alec spotted Julie standing next to Ben's headstone. He waved to her as he walked toward her.

"How did you know where to find me?" she said, holding a red rose.

"A guy's best man never forgets a wedding anniversary. When I didn't find you at home, I had a hunch you'd be out here. I was on my way to Rudy Johnson's place in Homestead, but I wanted to stop by to see how you were doing."

"I hope you have some good news." She dabbed her eyes with a handkerchief. "I don't know if I can keep coming out here, not knowing why he had to do this—to himself. To us."

"If it's any comfort, I think we're getting closer to finding that connection we talked about earlier. Turns out that Conway, the guy I went to see, committed suicide a few weeks ago. His widow didn't seem too broken-up over it, which I have to admit, surprised me a little."

Julie stared at him for a moment. "That confirms it then, doesn't it? All three have the same thing in common. The incident with the burning house fifteen years ago."

Alec nodded. "Now all we have to do is figure out what it's all about. So far we've got three dead ex-cops, a few clues and a lot of unanswered questions." He repeated everything Mrs. Conway had told him, including the fact she'd been planning to divorce him.

"Did she mention a letter, like the one Ben received?"

"She didn't, but frankly I don't think she cared enough about the guy to remember. Really sad."

"By the way, I went through Ben's papers like you suggested, but I didn't find anything. For the heck of it I went through the wastebasket next to his desk. Fortunately I hadn't emptied it. Anyway I didn't find much except a piece of paper with the name Victor with three questions marks next to it."

"Victor," Alec repeated. "The name doesn't sound familiar. Could be another ex-cop. I'll check it out."

Julie turned away for a second. "What are you going to do if Rudy Johnson turns out to be another suicide?"

He took a moment to answer. "I'm not sure. One thing I won't do is go to the police, not until I have something solid. Cops are skeptical by nature and they might not take it as seriously as they should. I've seen too many cases blown off simply because the facts weren't fully developed."

Julie waited a moment, and then placed the rose at the base of Ben's headstone. Turning to Alec she said, "Do you mind if I go to Johnson's place with you? It'll help take my mind off things." She shook her head. "It would have been our eighteenth anniversary."

He looked at her, nodding. "Yeah, sure. We can go in my car and I'll bring you back."

They drove to Homestead, a small farming town a little more than halfway between Miami and the Florida Keys. Johnson had lived there with his wife Alice since leaving the department.

"Let's keep our fingers crossed," Alec said, pulling into the long dirt driveway of the sturdy-looking coral rock house. The grass looked like it hadn't been cut in weeks.

They got out of the car, walked up to the door and tried the bell. No answer.

"Let's check with one of the neighbors," Alec said. They went across the street and knocked on the door. A moment later, a thin, bespectacled man with a dour look on his face opened the door.

"We're looking for the Johnsons across the street," Alec said. "You wouldn't happen to know if they moved or maybe went away on vacation, would you?"

A look of suspicion crossed the man's face. "Why are you looking for them?"

"We're old friends." Alec forced a smile. "Hadn't seen them in years. We wanted to surprise them and catch up on old times."

"I'm sorry, but I really can't help you. I mind my own business and don't pay attention to what people are doing, including my neighbors across the street." He stepped back to close the door.

"Well, just in case you do see them, can I give you my name and phone number?"

The man shrugged. "Sure, if you want."

Alec scribbled his name and phone number on a piece of paper and handed it to him. He took note of a gold Masonic ring on the man's right hand. "Thanks."

Alec tried to act natural as he and Julie ambled back to the car. "The guy was holding back on us," he said under his breath.

"How could you tell? He seemed okay to me."

Alec waited until they were inside the car. "The guy wore a Masonic ring. I recognized it only because Johnson wore one just like it. We razzed him a lot, the way Masons have their secret signs and all that stuff."

She turned to him with a puzzled look. "So they were both Masons. So what?"

"Maybe I'm wrong, but one thing I do know is that Masons are tight with each other, really tight, if you know what I mean. They're kind of like a secret fraternity. All for one and one for all, that kind of thing. They look out for each other, which I guess isn't altogether a bad thing."

"And you think that's what the man was doing, protecting him?"

"Two Masons living across from each other. Of course he was protecting him. They probably went to meetings together."

"Maybe I missed something but why would Johnson need protecting?"

Alec shook his head. "That's what I hoped Johnson would tell us." He cranked the engine and pulled away slowly.

"Well, at least we know Johnson didn't commit suicide," Julie said.

Alec nodded, but didn't say anything. He was just glad he didn't have to face another widow.

CHAPTER 7

"**C**hampagne?" said the young, ponytailed waiter who greeted Alec at the entrance.

"Thanks." He accepted a glass of Perrier Jouet. He took a quick sip and scanned the L-shaped gallery filled with an odd mix of collectors, students and wannabe socialites. Laura Conway spotted him from across the room and sauntered over to greet him. "I didn't think you'd show up," she said, smiling. She wore a sleek, black dress with a plunging neckline above which hung a small tear-shaped diamond. "But I'm glad you did."

He glanced at a familiar-looking painting on the wall next to where they were standing. "I see you finished it. What do you call it?"

"NO VACANCY. Just like the sign in front of the gates."

"Well, I don't know much about art, but I like it. I really do."

"We take cash, checks or credit cards." She grinned.

Alec leaned closer to read the price tag. "Thanks but I think I'll pass. Eight thousand bucks is just a little over my budget."

"Well, if you change your mind, I'm sure we can work something out. Come, let me show you around."

Alec set his glass on the table and allowed her to escort him around the room.

"This is my favorite." She faced a small painting that didn't look like any of her other works—a portrait of herself looking into a mirror. The reflection was a face at least ten years younger.

"I'm afraid I don't get it." He studied the two faces.

She sighed. "Of course not, you're a man. I was feeling a little down the day I painted it. It was my thirty-fifth birthday. Every woman dreads turning thirty-five. We all look in the mirror and wish we looked like we did when we were firmer, prettier and…well, you get the picture. I'll never sell it. My agent thinks I'm crazy because so many people have offered to buy it."

"Personally, I find the thirty-five-year-old face much more interesting." He stared at her for a second as if to confirm what he had just said.

"Thanks. I think." She stepped away from the painting, smiling. "So, did you come here just to see my wonderful paintings?"

"As a matter of fact, I *was* curious to see your work. But the truth is, there's something I wanted to ask you about a name that came up recently."

"What name?"

"Victor. He could have been an ex-cop or maybe a friend of your husband's"

"Victor. I don't know why but the name sounds vaguely familiar. Jeff had a lot of friends—cops, ex-cops, people that I never got to know personally. Why is he important?"

"It may be nothing but Ben's widow found his name on a piece of paper with three question marks next to it."

"If you want, I can check through my husband's papers. It'll give me an excuse to clean up his cluttered desk. I've been putting it off for too many days."

"That would be great." Alec handed her a piece of paper with his phone number on it. He spotted a bald, pudgy man with a camera coming toward them. "Well, I don't want to take anymore of your time. I'll see my way out." He started to back away slowly. "By the way, I really enjoyed your paintings."

She smiled and turned toward the pudgy man who walked up and gave her a quick peck on the cheek.

"Your work is marvelous as always, Laura," the man said. "Let's take a few shots with you in the forefront. Then we'll make our way around the gallery." He adjusted his lens and cocked his head to one side.

"Whatever you say, Walter." Laura struck a pose that made her look more like a model than a professional artist.

The next day, Alec dropped by the police department and talked to a few of his buddies, mostly old veterans, who'd been around since before he had left the department. None remembered a Victor, which meant that he probably wasn't a cop or even an informant. Disappointed, Alec left the station and took his time driving back to his apartment. Minutes later his phone rang and he answered it on the second ring.

"This may or may not be important," Laura Conway said, her voice tentative, "but I found a paper with the name Victor scribbled across it. I'm not sure whether—"

"Do you mind if I take a look at it, if it's not too much trouble?"

"Not at all. I'll put it aside for you."

"Thanks. I'll be there in thirty to forty minutes."

Laura answered the door wearing a baggy white shirt over a pair of faded jeans. She smelled of fresh rose petals as though she'd just taken a bubble bath.

"I hope you haven't eaten lunch." She led the way to the patio and to a table next to the pool.

"I usually skip lunch." He eyed the elegant setting: fresh flowers, crystal glasses, a platter of cold shrimp and smoked salmon and a bottle of wine.

"Well, maybe today you'll make an exception. I thought we'd have a snack while you look over the paper."

"Sure," he said, trying to be polite. They sat down simultaneously.

"Help yourself."

Alec hesitated, and then reached over to serve himself. "Tell me something." He smiled. "Do you prepare this kind of spread for all your visitors?"

"It's no big thing. It's lunch time and I hate to eat by myself." She picked up the bottle of wine and poured a little into each glass.

A moment later she grabbed a folder from the chair next to her and pulled out a sheet of paper. She handed it to Alec. "I really don't know what my husband was up to. They look like notes of some kind."

Alec studied the jumble of words.

VICTOR
Money - letters
Time running out - Victor or his friends
Leave the country - passport
Who can we trust?

"Looks like fast scribbling, like he was talking on the phone. Any idea who it could've been?" He took a quick sip of wine and looked at her.

"Like I said before, my husband had a lot of friends and I only knew a few of them. If he was in some kind of trouble, I certainly didn't know anything about it. It was just like him, to want to keep me in the dark, to want to protect me."

"From what?"

She shrugged. "From whatever it was that he was involved in, I suppose."

Alec read the note again, and then looked up at Laura. "Do you mind if I keep this?"

"It's yours. Just do me a favor. If you ever find out what this is really about, can you let me know? I may have stopped loving the guy, but I still want to know." She sighed.

Alec nodded. "Sure. As far as I'm concerned, you have as much right to know as Julie."

Laura smiled softly. "Thanks, I appreciate that." She poured herself some more wine and changed the subject. "Well, have you thought any more about buying one of my paintings? I still have a few from last night."

Alec started to laugh. "Sure, when I win the lottery."

Laura raised her glass. "Well then, to winning the lottery and all that goes with it."

"I'll second that." He lifted his glass.

CHAPTER 8

Two days later, Alec finally got lucky.

"I heard you were looking for me," Johnson said, his tone guarded.

Alec gripped the phone. "I'm Alec Santana. You might remember me from—"

"I know who you are, but I don't know if I can trust you. All the others are dead and I'm supposed to be next. That's what he's hoping for."

"You mean Victor?"

"If you know who he is, then you know the whole story." Brief silence. "Wait a minute. Nobody is supposed to know about him." He hung up.

"Damn it!" Alec slammed the phone down and shook his head. "I blew it." He started to walk away when the phone rang again. He turned and picked it up in mid-ring.

"Look, I know you're in trouble and if you'll give me a chance I think I can…"

"It's me, Julie. What's going on?"

Alec let out a sigh. "I thought it was Johnson calling me back."

"You talked to Johnson? What did he want?"

"I don't know, but he sounded desperate. I made the mistake of mentioning Victor and he got scared and hung up on me."

"Maybe he'll call back."

"Yeah, maybe, but I wouldn't count on it. Without knowing who this Victor is or why it spooked him, it's hard to say when or if I'll ever hear from him again."

"So what are you going to do? Victor is obviously someone people are afraid of, and we don't have a clue as to who he might be."

Alec nodded. "You're right. We don't know anything about him, except that he may have had some connection to Ben and Jeff Conway."

"Conway? What's the connection?"

"I'm not sure. Laura Conway called a couple of days ago after finding a piece of paper with some notes and Victor's name on it. I dropped by her house to check it out and it turned out to be nothing significant, at least nothing that made any sense. Laura was helpful but she didn't know anything, which didn't surprise me." He cleared his throat. "She's a remarkable woman. I can see why Jeff fell for her."

He heard a click from his call-waiting. "Maybe it's Johnson. I'll talk to you later." Double click. "Hello?"

"This is Brock. Can I speak to Deandra?"

"You got the wrong number." Alec dropped the phone in its cradle. Johnson never called back.

The next day, Alec went to see Johnson's neighbor, the Mason who lived across the street from him. When he rang the bell and no one answered, he went around the back and tapped on a sliding door window that had vertical blinds hanging freely. Through the slats, he saw the man moving about.

"I need to speak to you," Alec said. "It will only take a moment."

The man refused to answer.

"Look, I just want to ask you a question and then I'll be on my way."

The man stepped up to the sliding door, his lean face contorting into a scowl. "If you don't stop bothering me, I'm going to call the police. Now leave me alone and get the hell off my property."

"Just do me favor, please tell Johnson to call me again. It's very important that I talk to him."

The man picked up the phone. "I'm calling the cops." His finger was ready to punch the numbers. "You got ten seconds to leave my property. I mean it."

"Okay, okay." Alec backed off.

CHAPTER 9

"So what's this all about?" Alec said to Julie from across her kitchen table. "On the phone, you sounded a little mysterious." He dropped half a teaspoon of sugar into his coffee and stirred it slowly.

She put her hand over his. "The reason I called you over is because… how can I say this without sounding ungrateful for all you've done? I want you to back off."

"Is it because of Johnson? Look, I know you're disappointed, but I think the guy is looking for a lifeline, somebody who can help him, and sooner or later he'll call me again. I just know he will."

Julie shook her head. "That's what I'm afraid of. Whatever Ben was involved in, whatever it was that made him kill himself, is more than I can handle." She pursed her quivering lips. "I'm sorry, but I'd rather that you not pursue this any further."

Alec stared at her for a moment. "I've known you a long time, Julie, and something tells me you're holding back on me. You've changed your mind for a reason, a damn good reason. Am I right?"

Julie nodded, and then got up to finish taking the dishes out of the dishwasher and putting them in the cupboard. "Last night," she said, haltingly, "I had a long conversation with Ben's sister, Loretta. She and I are very close. In fact, she's like a sister. Anyway, we reminisced about the good times, the sad times and about a lot of things, trivial stuff, that meant so much to both of us. By the time we said goodbye, I knew in my heart that I couldn't do it. I couldn't risk hurting her and the rest of Ben's family by pursuing something that might reveal a troubled, perhaps darker, side of Ben."

Alec nodded but didn't say anything.

"As much as I want to know why Ben had to end his life the way he did, it may be best to leave well enough alone, for now at least. I hope you understand." She sniffled and swallowed back her tears.

Alec stood up. "It's your call, Julie. If that's what you want, then of course, I won't go any further." He forced a weak smile. "For what it's worth, I never had any doubt about Ben or the way things would turn out. In my book he was, and still is, one of the good guys."

"Thanks, Alec. I knew you'd understand. Ben was lucky to have you as a friend. And so am I."

"So what next—are you going back to your old job?"

"I don't think I'm ready just yet. Loretta invited me to spend a few days with her in Ohio. I'm thinking of taking her up on it."

"I think you should. It would do you some good. How long would you be away?"

"A week, maybe longer."

"Well, if you change your mind about anything, I'm just a phone call away." He reached over and kissed her on the cheek. "Stay in touch, okay?"

After leaving, Alec thought about what Julie had said. Maybe she was right. Maybe it was best to leave things as they were. Still, when he thought about Ben and all the questions yet to be answered, he hoped Julie might change her mind. He wouldn't count on it though, not with that pile of work waiting back in his office.

Minutes later he got a call from Cecil. "I got your papers back from Atlanta. They were able to bring up some more letters and a few of the words."

"Anything interesting?"

"There are no complete sentences, if that's what you mean."

"I might as well check it out. I'll be there in half an hour."

Alec held the papers taped together under the light. He took his time reading the words and letters. "Well, it's a little more than we had before."

lett ng y n that I av orma whi if ale uld be ve agin to you an our ami I'm talk out he one at you an the hers ol rom my ren use the ht he re. Yo oul ve ed he but y did Yo we all to usy rying to et the ney rom he t

　　So now me o ay for at you id. In act teen ays I w re what real ap ned fif s go. Every will now hat you re ust a ef, no be tha o on imin by am I iving ou ad ning, you mi ask? Well, I'd li e to ffer a ution. I'll with aling hat I now under on dit on. Tha ou o if On I know y av one you est sur at y r ec wil in a re

"I thought it might be a love note, or a poem," Cecil said.

"Or a complete waste of time." Alec said, sarcasm in his voice. "My friend Julie, the lady I was trying to help, wants me to stop the investigation, which means the note and everything I've uncovered will be put on hold indefinitely."

"You sound disappointed."

Alec frowned, nodding. "Yeah, I guess I am. But it was Julie's decision and I have to respect it." He glanced at his watch. "It's almost five thirty. Interested in a couple of beers?"

"You buying?"

Alec grinned. "I do owe you, don't I? Come on, let's get out of here."

CHAPTER 10

Barely awake, Alec heard a knock at the door. "This better be important," he mumbled as he got out of bed and put on his pants.

"Mr. Santana?" asked a young man wearing a dark blue shirt with a patch over his breast pocket that said Dependable Delivery Service.

"Yeah, what is it?" Alec scratched the back of his head.

"I have a package for you. Sign here, please." The young man handed him a clipboard with a delivery receipt, and then turned over a large, square-shaped package wrapped in brown paper.

Alec closed the door, carried the package into the living room and quickly unwrapped it. It was the painting of Laura looking into a mirror. He took a step backward just as the phone rang. He reached to answer it.

"So, do you still prefer the thirty-something face?"

He recognized Laura's voice. "I thought you said it wasn't for sale."

"It's not. It's a gift. You said you liked it, didn't you or were you just flattering me?"

"No. I mean yes, I like it but…"

"It's my way of saying thanks for being so understanding. You're the only one who hasn't made me feel guilty for not playing the grieving widow. For some reason everyone just assumed that Jeff and I were happily married. When I tried to explain the way things really were between us, well, let's just say nobody wanted to hear it."

"I don't know what to say except, thanks. I really appreciate it."

"If you want, I can give you the name of a good frame shop. They're the best in city."

"That'd be great." He reached for a pen and jotted the information on the back of a phone bill. "By the way." He hesitated on purpose. "The answer to your first question is *yes.*"

She laughed.

"I'll talk to you later. And thanks again for the painting."

"You're a lucky man," said the old man, his eyes darting between Alec and Laura's painting. "I never thought she'd sell it." He picked up samples from a wooden box and set them down along the edge of the painting.

"She didn't exactly sell it. It was a gift."

The man's dark eyes lit up. "Then you must be a very good friend. She's a special lady and a very talented artist." He shook his head. "It's terrible what happened to her husband."

"Did you know him well?"

"As a matter of fact, I'm the one who introduced the two of them. One day he brought in some old Civil War pictures he wanted framed. I'm a Civil War buff myself, so we struck up a conversation. After that, he'd drop by to chat or whenever he brought something in. He stood right where you are, the day Laura came to pick up a job I did for her. I knew both of them, so I introduced them. It must have been love at first sight because they were married six months later."

"Sounds like they were the perfect couple."

The man nodded. "Just days before he died, Laura brought in a small portrait of herself holding sixteen yellow roses, one for each year they had been married. She wanted it framed so she could give it to him for their anniversary."

"Their anniversary?"

"It was supposed to be a surprise." He sighed. "Jeff killed himself before she had a chance to give it to him."

Alec became quiet. "Well, I'm sure you're busy." He looked down at the samples. "If it were yours, which frame would you choose?"

The man thought about it for a second, and then picked up a sample with an antique finish. "I think this one would give it a classic look without overpowering the beauty of the two faces."

"You're the expert. When can you have it ready?"

"Why don't you pick it up in three days, anytime after one."

"Fine. I'll see you then."

CHAPTER 11

The phone rang when Alec entered his drab, cluttered office. He made his way to his desk. His first day at work in over two weeks, he was in no hurry to answer it.

"Aren't you going to get it?" said one the clerks, a plumpish, no-nonsense type of woman who wore her grayish-black hair in a bun.

"Yeah, sure, after I have my coffee."

It stopped ringing.

Alec carefully removed the lid from a large Starbucks coffee container, took a quick sip, and then set it down. "Did you miss me, Miriam?"

"Humph." She dropped a bunch of files on top of his desk. "The boss wants you to look these over. He wants them back by the end of the day."

The phone rang again. She glared at Alec, waiting for him to answer it. Frustrated, she picked it up. "Mr. Santana's office," she said very business-like. "Yes, just a minute." She handed the receiver to Alec. "It's a man calling about a picture frame. And don't forget what I said about the files." She turned around and hurried out of the office.

"Hello?" Alec said.

"Mr. Santana, this is Pablo from the frame shop. I just wanted to let you know your frame will be ready by the end of day."

"Great. That was quick. I'll be there around six."

⌒

Alec felt a light tap on his shoulder as he stood in front of the counter. He turned around. "Laura. What a surprise."

She smiled. "It sure is. I'm here to pick up some paintings I dropped off a couple of days ago." Her face lit up when she saw Pablo coming out of the back room holding Alec's painting. "I love it. I couldn't have picked a more perfect frame."

"It was Pablo's choice, but I agree. It looks great." He pulled out his checkbook and wrote a check.

"I'll get yours, Laura." Pablo disappeared into the back room. He came back shortly, carrying two of her paintings—a still life of flowers and candles and a life-like rendition of Adam and Eve in the Garden of Eden.

"They look great as always, Pablo. Just put it on my account."

"Sure thing, Mrs. Conway." He stepped to the side to help the next customer.

Laura hesitated. "If you don't have other plans, I know this little Thai place just up the street and, well, like I said before, I hate eating alone."

Alec grinned. "That's the best offer I've had all day. I'll follow you."

"I have a confession to make," Laura said, midway through the meal. Her tone was light, almost playful.

"Oh." Alec waited for her to continue.

"It wasn't a coincidence, the two of us being at the frame shop at the same time. When I checked to find out if my frames were ready, Pablo mentioned you had been by with your painting. I asked if he could put a rush on yours, which he did. And so I got there about the same time you did."

Alec smiled at her. "Are you always this honest with people you hardly know?"

She laughed. "Not always. The fact is, I didn't know when or if I would hear from you again and, well, it seemed like a harmless thing to do."

"Since we're being honest, I have to admit I was really glad to see you. I meant to call you, to thank you again for the painting, but I've had others things on my mind lately."

"Like the investigation into your friend's suicide—how's it going?"

"It's not." Alec shook his head. "Julie, Ben's widow, suddenly put an end to it. She's afraid there might be a skeleton or two in Ben's closet, which is crazy. Ben was a good friend. As far as I'm concerned, he was the last of the good guys."

"So what are you going to do?"

Alec reached for a glass of water and took a large gulp. "I've got no choice but to respect Julie's wishes. It's too bad, though. I was getting close to finding a connection between the ex-cops who killed themselves and this Victor fellow, whoever he is. Anyway, that's the reason I didn't call you and…why I'm feeling a little down."

She stared at him for a moment as though she were studying him. "I'd like to paint your portrait someday. You have an interesting face. Strong jaw line—very masculine." She half smiled. "Your hazel blue eyes and thick black hair with just enough gray makes you look…"

Alec laughed. "I hope you weren't going to say distinguished."

Laura chuckled. "That's not what I was going to say." She hesitated. "Do you like old movies, like from the fifties and sixties?"

"Yeah, sure," Alec said after a brief pause.

"I'm an old movie buff and just bought the latest DVD edition of *Zorba the Greek*. I was going to curl up on the couch, pop some corn, and check it out. Interested?"

Alec thought about it for a moment. "The last time I saw that movie was about twelve or thirteen years ago. For some reason, I don't remember the ending, but I do remember the scene where the guy played by Anthony Quinn tried to protect a woman from a mob that wanted to kill her."

Alec's pants lay on the floor and Laura's bra hung over the couch. It had been quick and intense, with almost no foreplay and even less conversation.

"I guess we missed the end of the movie." Alec sat up, still breathing hard.

Laura wore a contented look on her face and didn't say anything. After a moment, she got up, picked up her clothes and sauntered over to the bedroom. "Why don't you rewind the movie and pour us a drink while I freshen up?"

"Good idea." Alec put on his pants. He clicked the rewind button on the remote and let it run for about forty seconds. Then he walked over to a small, circular bar in the corner of the room and poured some cognac into two snifters. Leaning forward to grab some napkins, he spotted a painting that had been stuck upside down behind the bar.

Curious, he cocked his head to get a better look. It was the painting of the sixteen roses—the one she had planned to give to Jeff for their anniversary.

Laura came out of the bedroom wearing a different outfit, a pink linen shirt over a pair of white pants. "I thought I'd get into something more comfortable."

Alec handed her one of the snifters. "By the way, I saw your portrait with the roses behind the bar. What are you going to do with it?"

She took a sip of her cognac. "I don't know, maybe I'll donate it. It's certainly not one of my better works. To be honest, I don't even know why I painted it."

Alec frowned, slightly. "I thought…" He didn't want to repeat what Pablo had told him.

"Thought what?"

"I thought it looked familiar, somehow."

She smiled. "Let's see the end of the movie."

CHAPTER 12

When Alec opened the door, his friend Cecil stood there wearing a silly grin on his face. "I figured it out," Cecil said, walking into the apartment. He carried a bunch of papers rolled up in his hand.

"What are you talking about?" The clock on the wall said 11:51 p.m. "At this hour, it'd better be good."

"The note with the missing words and letters. I couldn't get it out of my mind, so I worked on it little by little. I'm pretty good with crossword puzzles and it occurred to me that it was just another kind of puzzle. That's when I—"

"So where is it?"

Cecil stepped up to the breakfast bar and dropped the papers on the counter. "These are my word combinations." He flipped through the first four pages. "You can see where I tried to fill in the blanks with every possible letter. There's a few that stumped me, but overall I think I got most of it." He paused, as if for effect, and then slowly pulled out the last sheet with the full message.

Alec picked it up and studied it for a long moment.

It read,

_____ *letting you know that I have information which if revealed would be very damaging to you and your family.* _____ *I'm talking about the money that you and the others stole from my parents' house the night of the fire. You could have saved them, but you didn't. You were all too busy trying to get the money from the attic.*

So now it's time to pay for what you did. In exactly ___teen days I will reveal what really happened fifteen years ago. Everyone will know that you are just a thief, no better than a common criminal. Why am I giving you advance warning, you might ask? ___I'd like to offer a solution. I'll withhold revealing what I know under one condition. That you take your own life. Once I know you have done it, you can rest assured that your secret will remain a secret.

"This is heavy, really heavy," Alec said, his eyes still fixed on the paper. "I can imagine what Ben must have gone through…what went through his mind." He looked up at Cecil. "This doesn't change a thing. I'm off the case. Julie told me to back off, and like it or not, I have to respect her wishes."

"But this is proof that Ben Brody was into something, something he couldn't control. Don't you want to know what it was?"

"Of course I do." Alec stepped back. "And so would Julie, under different circumstances." He rubbed the side of his neck. "Look, I appreciate you coming over to show this to me but I'll need some time to think about it."

"What's there to think about? This is the break you were looking for." He shook his head. "I just don't get it. You came to me for help and then when I put it all together, you tell me to forget it."

"You're right," Alec said after a moment. "I didn't even say thank you, did I?" He stroked his chin a couple of times. "What do you say if we meet for coffee at that Cuban place near my office tomorrow morning? We can talk some more. And, who knows, maybe I might even let you change my mind."

Cecil smiled. "That's more like it. I'll see you there at eight."

The waitress delivered an order of Cuban toast, and then poured *café con leche* into two cups.

"So, did you think about it?" Cecil said.

Alec looked around as if to make sure no one was listening. "After you left, I couldn't get the note out of my mind. I guess part of me didn't want to believe that maybe Ben was involved in something illegal. I still don't believe it because I knew Ben better than anyone." He sighed. "There's something about this that just doesn't make any sense."

"What do you mean?" Cecil reached for the bread, tore off a piece and dunked it into his coffee.

"Well, for instance, how does this guy know so much about what happened during that fire? And another thing, why didn't he ask for the money? I certainly would have, wouldn't you?"

"So, the guy doesn't want the money. Maybe he figures they already spent it. Look, the way I see it, the guy wants revenge, pure and simple. Right or wrong, he blames Ben and the others for the deaths of his parents."

Alec turned away for a moment. "You know, for the life of me I can't understand why Ben didn't say anything to me about this. We could've kicked it around and come up with something. Together we could have found a way to beat this. Maybe even expose whoever was behind it."

Cecil slurped his coffee. "I didn't know Ben that well, but even if part of what's in the letter is true, he would have been too ashamed to tell anyone, even you. It makes sense to me."

"Well, it doesn't to me," Alec said, almost shouting. "Not because he was my friend, but because I know Ben was solid as a rock. No matter what the letter says, I'm telling you he didn't steal any money and he certainly wasn't responsible for the deaths of two people."

Cecil motioned to him to keep it down.

"I'm sorry, but it just burns me when I think Ben killed himself over this stupid letter. If Julie ever found out about it…" He shook his head. "It would absolutely destroy her."

Cecil looked at him for a moment. "So, what are you going to do? I mean, now that you've had some time to think about it."

Alec picked up his cup and took a long sip. "I don't think I have any choice. The letter changed everything. There are just too many questions that need to be answered."

"I knew you'd come around." Cecil grinned. "So what next?"

"I might start by reviewing some old records about the fire and the deaths of the two people. Then I'll talk to a few of my old buddies from the P.D." He pulled out the letter and read it again. "Well, at least we know one thing we didn't know before."

"What's that?"

"The supposed motive behind the letter." He moved his chair back and stood up. "I've got to get going. I'm ten minutes late for a meeting."

"Go ahead, I think I'll stay and finish my coffee. Just don't forget to call if you find something interesting."

"You got it," Alec said, pointing at him.

The phone rang as Alec walked into his apartment and he rushed to answer it. "We need to talk," said a man with a shaky voice.

"Who is this?"

"My name is David Donahue, Johnson's neighbor. You came to my house several days ago."

"I'm listening."

"I think someone is trying to kill me. It's important that I speak with you, I'll explain everything when I see you."

"Where can we meet?"

"You know the Holiday Inn on South Dixie Highway—the one across from the University of Miami?"

"I know where it is."

"Meet me there in half an hour. I'll be in a red Toyota." He hung up.

Alec waited in the parking lot of the Holiday Inn for almost an hour. Donahue never appeared.

CHAPTER 13

"Just in from our mobile news unit," said the fast-talking host of the morning radio show. "Police are currently on the scene where sometime during the night, a man in a red Toyota drove into a canal off Alligator Alley near Southgate Boulevard."

Alec stopped at a light and reached to turn up the volume.

"The as-yet unidentified man was apparently unable to free himself and drowned in the deep canal. There were no skid marks, which according to police, would suggest the driver might have fallen asleep at the wheel. In a few minutes, divers will attempt to retrieve the submerged vehicle with the man's body still in it. Stay tuned for more details."

"Red Toyota," Alec whispered. His mind went over Donahue's phone call from the day before. Coincidence? Maybe. The light turned green and the driver behind him sounded his horn. Alec crossed the intersection, then turned around and headed in the direction of Alligator Alley.

When he got to the scene, divers were already in the water. They had hooked up the sunken car with steel cables from a winch on a tow truck and checked to make sure everything was secure.

"Okay, bring it up," shouted one of the divers, his head bobbing on the surface of the choppy water. The next moment, the cables became taut as the motorized winch began to turn slowly. Within minutes the entire car was out of the water and on dry ground. The medical examiner made a quick, almost cursory examination of the body still strapped in the driver's seat, and then signaled for attendants to remove it from the vehicle.

From behind a line of yellow tape, Alec watched as attendants moved the body to a waiting van. He could barely make out the man's face.

"I think I know the guy," Alec said to a young police officer on the other side of the tape. "I'll be glad to I.D. him for you."

"Wait here." The police officer walked over to where the medical examiner and a couple of detectives were standing. Seconds later, he waved to Alec, motioning him to come forward.

Alec lifted the tape and stepped under it, then hustled to the back of the van where the body lay. He took one look at the man's face and backed away.

"Yeah, that's him." He took a deep breath. "I only saw him a couple of times, but I'm sure it's Donahue."

"Donahue?" said one of the detectives.

"David Donahue. He lives—lived in Homestead." Alec gave the detectives what little he knew of Donahue, including details from the day before. They took his name and phone number and told him someone would call him.

A week later, Alec had yet to hear from anyone. When he read the morning paper, he found out the reason why. A short article on the local section described how the medical examiner had found large traces of alcohol in Donahue's blood. The official ruling: accidental death.

"Accidental my ass!" Alec threw the paper against the wall. He grabbed his coat from an easy chair and headed out the door.

"Look, I appreciate that you came to tell me this, but there's nothing I can do," Detective Palafox said. He stood next to an open filing cabinet. "See these files?" He ran his hand across the tops of dog-eared folders. "These are the unsolved cases where we know for sure the person was murdered. Like it or not, I've got to spend my time trying to solve them."

Alec hesitated, and then pulled out the copy of the deciphered note and handed it to Palafox. "This is the reason Ben Brody killed himself, and if I'm right, the reason Donahue was killed before he had a chance to tell me about it."

Palafox took a moment to read it. "This proves nothing." He handed the note back to Alec. "As far I'm concerned, it's all speculation."

Alec threw his arms in the air. "What do I have to do to convince you something is very wrong here? I'm telling you Donahue's death was no accident. The guy was scared shitless and he wanted to tell me something, only he never got a chance to do it."

Palafox closed the filing cabinet and walked over to his desk and sat down. He picked up a picture of himself standing in front of a small cabin in the mountains of North Carolina.

"See this cabin?" he said, his tone friendly. "That's where I want to be in ten months when I get my pension. If you had stayed on the force long enough you'd know where I'm coming from. To me, this is my little piece of heaven on earth and I'm not about to jeopardize it by digging into some wild-ass theory about something that happened a long time ago. The medical examiner ruled Donahue's death an accident, so who am I to question it? My advice to you is to forget it."

Alec clenched his jaw and held back from saying something he knew he'd regret. He knew Palafox's type: the kind who never worked past the end of his shift; the kind who always seemed to show up late to an officer's call for backup. Alec knew the type all too well, which meant that it would be a cold day in August before Palafox changed his mind.

"Well, I hope you have a good retirement." Alec's tone dripped of sarcasm. "If you change your mind, you know where to reach me."

CHAPTER 14

Three days later
"I tried calling you at your office, but they said you didn't work there anymore," Cecil said. "What's going on? You didn't get fired, did you?"

"I quit," Alec said, into his cell phone. He sat in his car, behind a white VW in the drive through lane of a savings and loan. "It's hard to explain, but this thing with Ben and the letter…well, it forced me into making a decision I should have made a long time ago."

"You found a better job?"

"Not exactly. The truth is, I'm going into business for myself. For a long time I've wanted to do something different, something that's not your typical nine to five gig. Ben's case gave me the push that I needed. It'll be tough the first few months, but my overhead is low and—"

"You're not talking about being a private investigator, are you?"

Alec chuckled. "You sound surprised, not that I blame you. I kept my old P.I. license from a few years ago when I first started thinking about it. I'm still a cop at heart, you know. I love working a good case and if I can make some money along the way, well all the better."

"What about Ben's case?"

"Ben's suicide is a priority and I want to finish what I started. After that, we'll just have to wait and see. By the way, let me tell you the latest." He filled him in on the details surrounding Donahue's phone call, his untimely death and Palafox's pissy attitude about the letter and the possibility that Donahue's death was no accident.

"You mean they're not doing anything with the letter?"

"It doesn't look like it. Palafox is ten months away from retirement. The only thing he has on his mind is his fucking ass, which he wants to protect, no matter what. He wouldn't lift a finger if there was even a remote possibility it might jeopardize his pension." The car in front of him moved forward. "Listen, I've got to hang up. I'll call you later, or better yet, why don't we meet at that bar near your office? You can buy me a beer to celebrate my new job." He laughed.

"Good idea. I'll see you there around six."

The next morning, Alec heard the doorbell ring and tried to ignore it. Seconds later, it rang again. "All right, all right," he mumbled as he sat up and got out of bed. He grabbed a robe from a hook on the wall.

He opened the door. "Laura." He brushed back his hair with his hand.

"Good morning, sleepy head." She looked bright-eyed and cheerful. She carried a large picnic basket, walked in and placed it on top of the breakfast counter. "I hadn't heard from you in a while, so I thought I'd surprise you. I've got warm croissants, fresh fruit, and a carafe of hot coffee." She smiled. "If you tell me you're a bacon and eggs man I'll..."

"As a matter of fact I am." He smiled. "But I'm not complaining."

Laura opened her basket and set out two place mats, pieces of fine china and silverware for two. Then she placed the fruit and croissants on a platter next to the setting. "Help yourself."

Alec scratched his head. "Room service at home. I'm impressed, I really am." He pulled out a stool and sat. Laura sat next to him.

They ate while they talked, at first about trivial stuff, and later about Alec's decision to become a private investigator. "I've decided to pick up where I left off with Ben's case. I hate going behind Julie's back on this but I feel that I have no choice. I have to see it through to the end."

A soft smile crossed Laura's face. "I've got an idea. Why don't you let me be your first client?"

Alec turned to her. "You're not serious, are you? Why would you need a P.I.?"

"Well, I don't really. What I had in mind was your friend's case. Since you're getting back into it, you could report to me rather than his widow. You said yourself that I had a right to know the truth, whatever it turned out to be."

Alec shook his head. "It wouldn't be right, taking money from a guy's widow, not under these circumstances."

"Well, then why don't we compromise? I'll pay your expenses. It's only fair I contribute something." She grinned. "I'm not exactly broke, you know."

Alec thought about it for a moment. "Okay, you got yourself a deal." He stood up and walked over to a desk on the other side of the room. He opened a drawer and pulled out a folder, then brought it back to the counter. "Why don't you read what's inside while I take a quick shower. It's the letter that the mysterious Victor sent to Ben and probably to Jeff."

Alec disappeared into the bedroom and came out ten minutes later wearing a blue polo shirt and a pair of tan Dockers.

"This is incredible." Laura held the letter in her hand. "If what the writer says is true, Jeff and the others had plenty of reason to be afraid."

Alec nodded. "You're right. Still, when I think of Ben, I can't help but wonder if there was something else going on here."

"What do you mean?"

"Well, I'm just not convinced Ben was a thief. Until I know for sure what really happened, I have to believe he was mixed up in something over which he had no control. Maybe he was framed."

"He was your friend. I can understand why you'd feel that way. To be honest, it's hard for me to believe Jeff killed himself because of something like this." She sighed. "Then again, maybe he felt he had no alternative."

Alec shrugged but didn't say anything, and then plopped himself on the couch. Laura walked over and sat next to him.

"Well, now that we're in this together," he said, his tone a little more serious, "let me bring you up to date." He repeated everything he had told

Cecil. When he was through, he got up and began to pace. "It's all connected. The note, the unexpected phone call from Johnson and now Donahue, whom the cops refuse to do anything about." He stopped pacing. "He was my only link to Johnson who's probably holed up somewhere, more afraid than ever to trust anyone, even me."

"So what are you going to do?"

"About Johnson?" He crossed his arms. "There's not much I can do, unless he calls again. Meanwhile I thought I'd do some research on Victor, now that we know who he is, more or less. At the time of the fire he was about eleven, which means he should now be in his mid-twenties. But before I do anything, I need to brush up on some of my old skills."

"What kind of skills?"

"Like the kind that might save my ass someday." He reached into a small canvas flight bag and pulled out a .38 Chief's Special. He opened and closed the cylinder to make sure it was empty, and then dry-fired it once, toward the ceiling. "I've got an old buddy, a retired cop, who owns an indoor range in Hialeah. I was planning on going over there this morning to shoot a few rounds. Want to come along?"

Laura shook her head. "I think I'll pass. Guns make me nervous." She stood to leave.

Alec grinned. "Somehow I knew you'd say that." He hesitated. "By the way, about the other night, I don't want you to think…" He cleared his throat. "What I'm trying to say is now that you're my client, maybe we should take it a little slower."

She smiled at him. "If that's the way you want it. Just keep me posted, okay?"

"You got it." He walked her to the door.

"Shooters, listen up," Mack bellowed from behind the line. "This is the last round. Ready on the right. Ready on the left. Commence firing."

Alec fired five rounds from his .38 Chief's Special, reloaded and fired five more. Seconds later, he heard a whistle blow and he set down his weapon. Even from twenty yards he could see where the bullets had struck. All but one had hit near the center of the target.

"I see you haven't lost your touch," said Mack, a short, middle-aged man with a G.I. haircut and a crooked smile. "How long has it been? Two, three years?"

"Would you believe four?"

"That long? Well, I hope this means you're back. Hey, what's this I hear about you being a private eye?"

Alec smiled. "Word sure travels fast. Actually, I haven't really started. I plan to take it slow and easy, at least in the beginning." He dropped his gun in a canvas bag. "I just thought of something. Didn't you work in records after you took a round in your shoulder? The reason I'm asking is because I'm researching an old case and thought you might know someone who'd be able to help me. If it pans out I'll tell you all about it."

Mack thought about it for a second, and then said, "Irene Bailey. She's been in records for many years and probably knows more about what's in those files than any detective in the department. I heard she just got promoted, getting ready to transfer to another unit. So you'd better see her soon. Tell her that I sent you."

Irene Bailey was a short, sturdy-looking black woman with a ready smile and a better than average memory of events from cases long since forgotten. She remembered the case about the Christmas eve fire and had no difficulty locating an old file.

"Do you mind if I look through it?" Alec said, from across her desk.

Irene hesitated. "Ordinarily, I'd ask you to submit a formal request." She started to shrug, then pushed the file toward him. "Oh, go ahead, it's an administrative file. There's not much in there anyway. If you don't mind, I've got a meeting to attend." She stood to leave. "When you finish just leave it on my desk."

"Thanks."

She was right. The file didn't contain much—a few newspaper clippings, two or three internal memos and an incident report by an arson investigator. One of the memos mentioned the names of the deceased and the sole survivor, a young boy named Victor Cardini. They were from Argentina and lived in Miami less than a year, with no known relatives in this country.

A handwritten post script on one of the memos, dated a week later, revealed that a family member had taken the boy back to Argentina. It appeared the fire had been viewed as nothing more than a tragic incident. The case was summarily closed.

Alec took a few notes, then closed the file and left it on Irene's desk along with a short thank you note that he stuck to the corner of the folder.

CHAPTER 15

*O*keechobee, Florida

"Get away from that window!" Johnson yelled at his wife.

He sat at the kitchen table, gulping shots of whiskey and thinking about his friend, Donahue, convinced his death was no accident. Maybe they had forced him to reveal where he and his wife were hiding. Maybe Victor and his friends were in the woods just waiting for him to step outside so they could shoot him. Well, he wouldn't make it easy for them. He had a loaded .357 Magnum, ready to shoot first and ask questions later.

His wife Alice paced, ignoring Johnson's request for her to sit down and do something…anything but complain as she'd done since they got there.

She stopped pacing. "I think we should pack up and leave. If I have to spend one more day holed up in this dump, I'm going to explode. And it won't be pretty."

Johnson gulped another shot. "We'll leave when I say so and not before." He caught a hard look from her and softened his tone. "Look, we'll give it 'till the end of the week and then—"

"Then what? Move to some other rat hole? I think it's time we went to the police. At least they'd be able to give us some protection. It's been fifteen years, for God's sake. What can they possibly do to you?"

Johnson slammed his fist on the table. "No cops and that's final. So far, nobody knows anything about this and I want to keep it that way."

"What about Santana? Maybe you should call him again. He's not a cop and all he wants to do is clear Ben Brody's name. Even Donahue suggested that you talk to him."

Johnson shook his head. "I don't trust him. Even when we were on the force together, I didn't trust him. It was a mistake for me to have called him."

"Well, then, what are you going to do? We can't keep hiding forever and we sure as hell can't go back to Miami."

Johnson knew his wife was right. He'd been thinking about it a lot and had already decided to do something he swore he'd never do: leave the country.

"I didn't want to tell you just yet." He hesitated. "But I know this guy, a snitch who can prepare false documents for us, driver's license, social security cards, birth certificates…the works. I thought about calling him so he can send us whatever we need in case we have to leave the country on a moment's notice. It would only be temporary. Once everything blows over, we could move to California or maybe Oregon."

She put her hands on her hips. "You really think this thing is going to blow over? The guy's a killer; he's not going to give up that easily. He's determined to see you dead." She sighed. "Sometimes I wish you'd never told me anything about it."

Suddenly the phone rang. They stared at it until it stopped ringing.

"Nobody's supposed to have this number." Johnson stood up and stepped toward the phone. "Maybe they know we're here. Maybe—"

The phone rang again. "I think we should answer it," his wife said. "It could be just a wrong number."

Johnson looked at her, nodding. "Okay, you get it. If it's them they'll know my voice."

"Hello?" She held her breath for a second.

"I'm trying to confirm an order," said the caller, a man with a foreign accent. "Did you order a pepperoni and mushroom pizza?"

"You got the wrong number. We didn't order a pizza." She hung up the phone and stared at Johnson. "The guy had an accent. Could've been Spanish. It was hard to tell."

"Damn it. Now I wish you hadn't answered it." He hesitated for a moment, then stepped across the room and pulled out a suitcase from under the bed.

"What are you doing?"

"What does it look like I'm doing? Start packing. We're getting the hell out of here."

She sighed. "It's okay with me. I was never a deep woods person anyway."

Alec stood in the kitchen, ready to heat up some leftover chili. The phone rang; he picked it up on the first ring. "It's good to hear your voice again. When did you get back?"

"Late last night," Julie said. "I wish I had stayed longer. But like it or not, I have to pull myself together and get back among the living, so to speak."

"I'm glad to hear that."

"By the way, when I got to Loretta's house, there was a letter waiting for me from Ben, postmarked the day before he died. I'm not sure why he sent it there. Maybe he assumed I'd be there. For a moment I was afraid to open it, but I'm glad I did."

"What did it say?"

"He didn't provide a reason for taking his life, if that's what you want to know. It was…very personal and…" She sniffled a couple of times. "Maybe we should leave it at that."

"I'm sorry. I shouldn't have asked."

"It's okay. As a matter of fact he mentioned you a couple of times. He asked to relay a message to you. Hold on. I've got the letter in front of me."

Brief pause. "Here it is. He wanted you to know that Rosario holds all the answers."

"Rosario," Alec repeated. "It doesn't ring a bell. Could be someone we used to know. Did he say anything else?"

"That's it. I can only assume it had to do with whatever was troubling him. Not that it matters anymore. I'm comfortable with my decision to let things stay as they are, at least for now."

"I understand," Alec said after a brief silence. "Hey, what do you say if I pick you up and take you to dinner? Nothing fancy, maybe Cuban sandwiches and beer or whatever you're hankering for. I'll tell you all about my job, my new job that is."

"Sounds great."

"Good. I'll pick you up in half an hour."

On the way to Julie's house in Dania, Alec had the uneasy feeling he was being followed. A black truck had been trailing from a distance. When he spotted the Sheridan Street exit up ahead, he slowed down and put on his blinkers. A second later the truck barreled past the exit and he breathed easy.

CHAPTER 16

The next day, which was Saturday, Alec got an early morning call from his friend, Cecil. "I know it's short notice," he said, "but a guy I work with loaned me his air boat for the day. He keeps it at a place near the Miccosukee reservation. Are you interested?"

"Yeah, sure, why not? I need to talk to you anyway. There's been a new development with Ben's case and I thought you might have some ideas."

"Good. You can tell me about it on the way out there. I'll pack some sandwiches and you bring the beer."

Alec hesitated. "You sure you know how to drive the damn thing?"

Cecil laughed. "Just be at my place in an hour. We'll go from here."

"It's almost as if Ben assumed you'd be looking for answers," Cecil said to Alec from behind the wheel of a blue Taurus. They drove west on the two lane road that cut through the everglades. "What about the woman—Rosario? Do you know anything about her?"

Alec shook his head. "Not a thing. I can't remember ever meeting anyone with a name remotely similar. At first I thought it might be an informant, or someone I had interviewed, but now I'm not so sure."

"Well, whoever she is, we have to assume she's connected to Victor Cardini. Don't you agree?"

Alec shrugged. "I don't know. Maybe. That's what makes it so frustrating. If only Ben had given me just a little bit more to go on. But maybe he didn't want Julie to know what he was involved in and figured that I'd know what he meant."

They were a little more than halfway between Miami and the Miccosukee reservation when Cecil, who'd been checking his rearview mirror, said, "A black truck has been tailing us for the past ten miles. Check it out."

Alec looked into the side mirror, then turned around. "We got trouble. It looks like the truck that was following me last night on I-95."

"Are you sure?"

"Well, there's only way to find out. Floor it, and I mean now. Go! Go!"

Cecil pressed the pedal and the car shot forward, quickly reaching 80 miles per hour. The truck stayed with them.

When they reached a slow moving car ahead, Cecil slowed the Taurus. They stayed behind the car for almost a mile, then Cecil suddenly accelerated and swung around it. The truck did the same and the chase was on again.

"The guy's nuts," Cecil said. The truck gained on him. "What's he trying to do?" A second later, they felt a jolt as the truck rammed their bumper.

The truck rammed them two more times, and then pulled alongside. Through the truck's darkened windows, all they could see was a hooded man wearing sunglasses.

Suddenly, the truck swerved into the Taurus. There was a crunch of metal as the door caved in.

"Speed up, speed up!" Alec yelled.

Cecil drove faster, but the truck stayed close.

In the distance, a yellow car traveled toward them. The truck waited until the last moment before pulling back. Then it quickly resumed its position alongside the Taurus. Again it slammed into the car. A second later, it sped up and moved in front of them.

Without warning the truck's driver slammed on his brakes. Cecil's car swerved to the right and skidded out of control. It flipped over three times and came to rest upside down on the opposite side of the road. Dazed and in pain, Alec looked for a way to free himself. He moaned as he turned to Cecil who seemed unresponsive.

Seconds later, the truck made a fast U-turn and sped away toward Miami.

When paramedics arrived, they found Alec still strapped to his seat. Cecil was out cold—blood oozed from his mouth and his nose. He'd suffered a severe blow to the head. They were rushed to a hospital in Miami.

Alec sustained only a couple of bruised ribs and a broken finger. He was treated and released the same day.

CHAPTER 17

Three days later Cecil still lay in a coma, his condition guarded. Doctors were reluctant to say when, or if, he'd come out of it.

"Thanks for meeting me here," Alec said to Laura from across a table in the hospital cafeteria. "I meant to call you sooner but with Cecil in this condition, well, I just wanted to do what I could for him and his family. His wife is with him now. Susan and I both come here everyday, hoping for the slightest bit of good news, but so far there's been no change."

Laura sipped her coffee. "On the phone you said something about a black truck. What was that all about?"

"I think someone tried to send me a message. The truck was the same one that followed me the night before. If my theory is correct, it's the same guy who ran Donahue off the road into a canal."

"Did you see the driver?"

Alec shook his head. "The windows were too dark."

"You think it was Victor?"

"It sure seems that way." He reached for his cup and took a quick sip. "It's like he's trying to eliminate anyone who might interfere with his sick blackmail scheme."

"Well, if you ask me, I'd say it's time to drop the investigation. It's certainly not worth risking your life over. Next time you may not be so lucky."

Alec took a deep breath. "I thought about that, but until I know what this whole thing is all about, I'm hanging in there. I'll be more cautious, though, especially when I'm on the road." He looked at her for a moment. "Just to be on the safe side, you might want to do the same."

Laura's eyes widened. "You really think I'll be in danger?"

"If you'd asked me that on Friday, I probably would've said no. But after what happened on Saturday, I'd rather not take any chances. Just stay alert and keep an eye for anything suspicious, or unusual. And speaking of unusual, does the name Rosario mean anything to you?"

"Rosario." The vowels rolled off her tongue as she repeated the name. "I can't say it does. Who is she?"

"That's what I'm trying to figure out. In a letter that Ben wrote to Julie right before he killed himself, he sent me a message. He wanted me to know that Rosario held all the answers." He looked away for a second. "Ben was trying to tell me something, but he didn't want to come right out with it. He must have assumed I'd figure it out."

From the hallway, a speaker suddenly blared, "Code arrest. Code arrest. Room 423."

Alec jumped to his feet. "That's Cecil's room!"

They rushed off the elevator. Personnel were rushing into Cecil's room. Seconds later, a doctor yelled, "Clear," and pressed the paddles over Cecil's chest. The heart monitor showed no response. Again the doctor yelled, "Clear," and gave Cecil another jolt. He did it three more times until someone finally said, "It's no use. He's gone."

"The hell he is," Alec said, coming up from behind. "Try it again."

The doctor looked at him. "You're not supposed to be in here," he shouted. He turned to one of the male nurses. "Get him out of here."

"Try it again, goddammit. That's my friend lying there and you're not going to give up on him. Do you understand?"

The doctor froze.

"I said try it again," Alec yelled. "We're wasting time."

"Okay, okay." The doctor slapped the paddles on Cecil's chest one more time and stood back. The line on the monitor remained flat. He tried it again and shook his head. "I'm sorry."

The monitor started to bleep; a nurse uttered a gasp. "He's back. He's back."

The doctor and his team went back to work on Cecil. When Alec saw that his friend would make it, he joined Laura in the hallway. "I could use a drink right about now.

Laura nodded and reached for his hand. "You've earned it."

CHAPTER 18

Alec hadn't checked his phone messages since the day of the accident. When he finally got around to it, he went through them quickly and paused hearing Irene Bailey's voice. "I just wanted you to know that I found more information regarding the case you came to review. Tomorrow is my last day, so if you want to look it over, you'd better come by pretty soon." She had left the message early yesterday morning.

Alec glanced at his watch. It was almost four o'clock. If he hurried, he had just enough time to catch her before she punched out for the day.

"If you had showed up a half hour later, I would've been gone," Irene said, from behind her desk.

He took a seat. "I'm sorry, but I was in a car accident a few days ago and things have been kind of hectic."

"You all right?" He grimaced and nodded as he touched the side of his chest. "So what do you have?"

She handed him a folder. "There's a memo in there and an evidence envelope that apparently had been misfiled. I found them by accident in another file I happened to be reviewing."

Alec opened the folder and read the memo written by a detective named Ray Leblanc. He had arrived at the scene long after the young boy had been rescued. The memo explained how and where the items were found. They were supposed to have been returned to the family, but no one ever showed up to claim them.

Alec opened the legal size envelope and poured out its contents: family photographs, old bills, miscellaneous receipts, some canceled checks, and a map of Argentina.

"Did you know Detective Leblanc?"

"Yes, but not well. He retired from the Department about two years ago. He used to live in North Miami Beach, not far from Laurenzo's Italian Market. But that was years ago." She glanced at a clock on the wall. "I hate to be a spoiler, but I still have some things to do before I call it a day. If you want you can keep the stuff in the envelope. Most of the non-essential files from that period were going to be destroyed within the next couple of months anyway."

"Thanks, I appreciate it." He placed the items back in the envelope and stood to leave. "You've been very helpful. If there's ever anything I can do for you, anything at all, don't hesitate to call me."

Irene thought about it for a second, then said, "As a matter of fact, there is something you can do for me." She hesitated. "It's a personal matter and I feel a little awkward just talking about it. But I've made up mind and I want to see it through." Her lips began to quiver.

"Take your time." He sat back down.

"When I was eighteen, I had a baby girl I was forced to give up for adoption. It was my parent's idea and I reluctantly went along with it. Later, after I married and had kids, I tried to put her out of my mind, but of course I couldn't. For a long time I had been thinking about hiring a private investigator to find her, and seeing as how you happen to be one, well…" She shrugged. "Will you do it, Mr. Santana? Will you help me find my daughter?"

Alec looked at her for a moment. "You sure you want to do this? I've heard a lot of stories about these reunions. Sometimes everything turns out all right but more often than not…" He shook his head. "Well, you know what I'm trying to say."

"I've thought about that and I'm prepared to take the risks. If I don't do it now when I have the chance, there's a good possibility I won't do it at all."

Alec nodded. "Okay. I'll need as much information as you can give me—date and place of birth, adoption papers, that kind of thing. When you get it all together, why don't you give me a call."

"I'm way ahead of you." From a drawer she pulled out an oversized envelope and handed it to him. "It's all in there, including some old information about her adoptive parents."

"I'll sure give it my best. Where can I reach you?"

Irene picked up a piece of paper and jotted down her address and phone number. "Call me the moment you find something." She slid the paper toward him.

"Give me three or four days. I should have some preliminary information for you by then." He stood up and smiled at her. "By the way... congratulations on your promotion."

Through an internet locator, Alec found last known addresses for the adoptive parents, Robert and Jane Halverson. He also found current information on Ray Leblanc. He didn't know what, if anything, Leblanc would be able to tell him, but he planned to find out.

Laurenzo's Market was busy even at nine in the morning. It was there, in the café section, that Leblanc had chosen to meet. The aroma of freshly brewed coffee and warmed over pastries clung to the air.

Alec spotted Leblanc, who said he'd be wearing a red polo shirt, sitting at a corner table. Alec introduced himself and sat across from him. "Thanks for meeting me. It's been a long time since I've been here. You come here often?"

"Almost everyday, except Sundays." Leblanc had the look of a cop who'd stayed on the force longer than he should have. "When I was still working I had lunch here at least once a week. Now that I'm retired, I come here mostly in the mornings. I have my coffee, read the paper, and sometimes run into old friends." He took a sip of his cappuccino. "So what can I do for you?"

"I'm looking into an old case—the one where a young boy was rescued from a burning fire fifteen years ago. I understand you showed up at the scene and I thought you might remember something that didn't appear in the file. My friend, Ben Brody, was one of the cops who responded. He committed suicide, you know?"

"I heard."

"Well, Ben's widow thinks his suicide was connected to what happened that night." Alec didn't want to divulge more than he had to, at least not until he was sure he could trust him. "I know it wasn't an active investigation, but do you remember anything about the boy's family? Anything at all?"

"To be honest, I had almost forgotten about it. Sure, I remember the fire and the news coverage that followed, but that's about it. Like you said, it wasn't an active investigation, at least not a criminal one."

"Let me throw a name at you. Rosario. Ever heard of her? She could've been the kid's sister or some other relative." Alec studied Leblanc. He could tell by the way he kept looking around that he really didn't want to be there.

Leblanc took a long sip of his coffee. "I'm not sure, but I seem to recall that someone—I don't remember who—mentioned the name right after the fire. The only reason it stuck in my mind was because at the time a Honduran girl named Rosario babysat for my daughter. Obviously whoever she was or whatever she had to do with the kid's family was not that significant, otherwise I'd know more about her."

Alec sighed. "Well, it was a long shot, but I'm glad I got to meet you. If you think of anything that can help—a name, a place or whatever, can you give me a call?"

"I'll be glad to."

Alec gave him his card and shook his hand, then got up and left.

Leblanc waited until he was sure Alec was out of the store, then got up and walked over to a pay phone near the exit door. He muttered something as he dialed a number he knew from memory. Seconds later, he hung up and went back to finish his coffee.

∽

After leaving Laurenzo's Market Alec drove over to the adoptive parents' residence in Carol City. When he got there he found out they had moved out over two years ago. According to one of the neighbors, a chatty, middle-aged woman with a Haitian accent, the Halversons had divorced. Mr. Halverson had run off with a younger woman and Mrs. Halverson had gone back to live with her mother who lived in a duplex in Opa-Locka, nearby.

"I don't know the address," the woman said, "but you shouldn't have any trouble finding it."

"How is that?"

"The house is bright yellow and it's right across from the City Hall complex. You know, the buildings that look like an Arabian castle."

Alec nodded. "I know the ones you mean." He looked at her for moment. "By the way, did you know their daughter?"

"Why do you want to know—is she in some kind of trouble?"

"No, nothing like that. Just curious." He didn't want to press his luck. She'd already told him what he needed to know.

CHAPTER 19

The Haitian woman was right, almost. The yellow house sat across the street, but a block away from the City Hall complex. Alec rang the bell and followed it with a knock. He heard footsteps, and then the door open slightly.

"Are you the insurance man?" said a forty-something woman. She had a small, fine-featured face and wore her long, salt and pepper hair combed to the back with a simple tie-back.

"No. I'm a private investigator and I wonder if I can speak to you."

"We've been waiting for days." She sighed. "Someone was supposed to come out here to check on the water damage from the last rainfall." She looked at him. "Who did you say you were?"

"My name is Alec Santana and I'd like to ask you a few questions about Sharon Halverson. May I come in?"

The woman hesitated. "You're not here to give me bad news about her, are you? Because if you are, I don't want to hear it. She's my daughter and I love her but—"

Alec raised his hand. "I can assure you it's nothing bad. I'll explain everything. It'll only take a moment."

The woman stared at him for a second. "Okay, come inside." She opened the door wider and allowed Alec to enter. They took a seat in the living room across from each other.

Alec looked around: framed family photos on top of the mantel, on the walls, and on small tables on either side of the couch. In the corner, an antique hutch filled with dozens of miniature dolls with dark, little faces and bright colored costumes.

"Interesting collection," Alec said, his eyes fixed on the hutch. "Are they yours?"

"They belong to my daughter. She started collecting them when she was in junior high. It seems like such a long time ago. She's only nineteen, you know."

Alec nodded. "I was hoping to speak to her about her birth mother. She hired me to find your daughter. I know this is all unexpected, but do you think your daughter would be interested in a reunion?"

The woman sighed. "I probably shouldn't be telling you this, but I haven't seen my daughter in over a year. She ran off with her friends. I have no idea where you can find her. She's been a headstrong girl almost from the day we got her. My husband and I…we did the best we could." She turned away to hide her tears. "I'm sorry, Mr. Santana, but all this brings back a lot of memories."

"I understand." Alec waited a moment, and then got up and dropped a business card on top of the coffee table. "If you should happen to hear from her, can you give her my number?"

The woman sniffled. "I will. But I can tell you that it won't do any good. She resents her birth mother for giving her up and she resents me too. I'm not sure why, exactly. We did the best we could, but I guess it wasn't good enough."

"If it's not too much trouble, can you show me a recent picture of her?"

The woman hesitated, then stood and went to one of the bedrooms. She came back holding a picture.

"It was taken the year she graduated from high school. You can have it, if you like. I've got another one."

Alec gazed at it. "She's got a pretty smile and she looks a little bit like her birth mother. Thank you."

On a hunch, Alec checked police and court records and found out that Sharon Halverson, also known as Sherri Anderson, had twice been arrested for prostitution within the past nine months. Both arrests had occurred late in the evening in the city of Miami near the intersection of Biscayne Boulevard and 79th Street.

From the courthouse, Alec called Irene to let her know what he'd found. He told her about his meeting with Mrs. Halverson and her feeling that Sharon would probably not want to meet her.

"There's something else." He hesitated. "I found out that Sharon had been arrested…for prostitution. I'm sorry, but I thought you should know." He gave her a moment. "I guess that's it, then. Under the circumstances, there's not much more we can do."

"You sound as if it's all over. As far as I'm concerned, nothing has changed. She's still my daughter and I'm not giving up that easily. Not after all these years."

Alec gave a heavy sigh. "You realize the odds are against you. And that's if I'm lucky enough to talk to her." He paused. "But if that's what you want, well, I'll just have to go out and find her. It may take a while, so if you don't hear from me, don't think I'm ignoring you."

"I understand. Just call me the moment you know something." Her voice broke. "Thank you Mr. S-santana. Thank you for not giving up on my daughter."

Back in his car, Alec picked up an incoming call.

"You just don't know when to quit, do you?" Detective Palafox said in a semi-monotone.

"What are you talking about?"

"I heard you've been poking around. I don't know what you're expecting to find, but you're meddling in something that doesn't concern you."

"Yeah, well, things have changed. I'm a private investigator now and I have no intention of backing off."

"Look, I thought I made it clear the last time we talked. There's no active investigation in this matter and there isn't going to be one. Do I have to spell it out for you?" Brief pause. "By the way it's too bad about your friend, Cecil. If I didn't know better, I'd say someone tried to send you a message." He chuckled.

"If you had something to do with that, I swear to God I'll—"

The line went dead.

"Son-of-a-bitch." He dropped the phone on the seat.

Alec spent the evening cruising Biscayne Boulevard looking for Sharon Halverson. Of the dozen or so hookers that he saw, none fit Sharon's general description. Most were either too old or white.

He pulled into the parking lot of a fast food restaurant, got out, and began to stroll. Just ahead, he spotted a black, heavy-set hooker wearing a beige tank top and tight-fitting shorts. She stood across the street from an adult theater and ran her hand near her crotch every time a patron came out. When she noticed Alec walking toward her, she paused and waited for him to approach her.

"You looking for a date, sugar?" she said, smiling.

"Sorry, not tonight." Alec pulled out a photo of Sharon and showed it to her. "She calls herself Sherri…Sherri Anderson. Ever seen her before?"

"Maybe, maybe not. You a cop?"

Alec shook his head. "I'm just trying to help somebody out." He pulled out a twenty-dollar bill and looked around to make sure it was safe. The last thing he needed was to be arrested for solicitation. "So, have you seen her?"

She grabbed the bill from his hand and tucked it into her bra. "The bitch used to come around, but not anymore. My man ran her skinny little ass out of here. Last I heard she was working the strip just north of the Fort Lauderdale airport."

"Thanks, thanks a lot." He backed off.

CHAPTER 20

*M*idmorning

"Who is this?" Alec said into the receiver.

No answer.

"Who is this?" he repeated.

"Rudy doesn't know I'm doing this," said the caller, a woman with soft a Georgia accent. "But he's desperate and he's doesn't know what to do or who to trust. I wish I could tell you more." She was quiet a moment. Alec wondered if she'd hung up. "The truth is, I don't know how much more I can take of this hiding and running from something or someone that we don't know anything about."

"Look, I have a fair idea of what's going on here, and I think I can help. Is there any way you can convince your husband to talk to me? Maybe he and I can figure something out. Sooner or later he has to trust someone. You know that, don't you?"

"Yes, I know, but he's gotten it into his head that everyone is against him. Even you, which I don't really understand."

"Well, then, what are you going to do? He's the last of the four cops and time is running out. This guy Victor, is not only sick, but he's unpredictable. There's no telling where or when he'll show up next."

In the background, a door clicked shut. "I've got to go," she whispered. "My husband's back. I'll call you later."

"Wait..."

She had already hung up.

Afraid he might miss a call, Alec hung around the apartment the rest of the day. Every time the phone rang, he rushed to answer it, but it was always someone else. Frustrated, he grabbed his keys and drove over to the strip on U.S. 1 to look for Sharon Halverson.

He saw a few hookers, none that resembled Sharon. According to a clerk in a convenience store just north of the Fort Lauderdale airport, the area was "hot," meaning that cops were making regular busts for prostitution. Alec showed him Sharon's picture.

"She looks vaguely familiar," the clerk said, "but after a while they all kind of look alike, if you know what I mean. Personally, I think they ought to legalize it."

Alec put the photo away. "Thanks."

After leaving the store, he drove up and down the street a few more times, and then pulled into a taco place for a burrito and a beer. He sat at a booth facing the rear.

"Hello, stranger," said a woman's voice from behind. Her tone was light, almost playful.

Alec turned around. "I'm impressed." He smiled. "I really am." She wore a sheriff's deputy uniform. "When did this happen?"

"About four years ago. It was right after we last saw each other, in fact." She sat down across from him.

"Has it really been that long? I guess it has. Look Bonnie, about that night…"

She smiled. "Forget it, maybe you did me a favor. It gave me the kick in the pants I needed. So, how about you? What have you been up to?"

A waitress delivered a complimentary cup of coffee.

"Thanks, Maggie," Bonnie said.

"I'm a private investigator. I just started so it's still new to me." He stared at her for a second. Her dark, curly hair was shorter and she wore no makeup, which made her look almost plain. "In case you're wondering, I'm still single. And you?"

"Well, I married a cop from another department—it's hard to attract civilians, you know. But it didn't last. Two cops in the family is a bit much, I discovered. Our job was all we ever talked about, that was when we were lucky enough to see each other. One day we both agreed it wasn't working out. We're still friends, though. I can count on him for anything."

"No kids, I take it."

She shook her head. "That's another reason we split up. I wanted a baby and he didn't. It was his second marriage; you know how that goes. He already had two kids." She took a sip of her coffee. "So, are you just hanging out?"

"As a matter of fact, I'm working a case. I'm trying to find a girl who was given up for adoption nineteen years ago. Her mother hired me to find her." He pulled out Sharon's photo and dropped it in front of her. "She's a hooker and she may be working the strip."

Bonnie picked up the photo. "You know, she looks like a girl I used to see now and then. But that was months ago. If it's the same one, she got pregnant by one of her Johns, I would guess. It didn't stop her from working the strip, though—that is until she couldn't hide it anymore."

Alec reached for his beer. "I had a feeling it wasn't going to be easy. You think she's still in the area?"

"Probably." She shrugged. "If you want, I'll ask around. I'll call you if anything turns up."

"I'd appreciate it." They exchanged phone numbers. He hesitated. "Do you mind if I call you sometime, for dinner, a movie or whatever?"

She had to think about it. "To tell you the truth, Alec I don't think—" A call suddenly came through her radio.

"Robbery in progress at a convenience store near the corner of Davie Boulevard and Southwest Nineteenth Avenue. Shots fired, shots fired. All available units please respond. Approach with caution."

Bonnie's light mood faded. "Sorry, but I have to go." She stood to leave. "It was nice seeing you again. I'll call you if I find anything on your girl, Sharon."

CHAPTER 21

A week later, Alec had yet to hear from anyone, including Laura. On his way to visit a new client who had been referred to him by his friend, Mack, he swung by her house and spotted what looked like an unmarked police car sitting in the driveway. He drove around the block and parked at the end of street.

Minutes later Detective Palafox came out of the house. Alec waited for him to get in his car and drive off.

"Hi Alec," Laura said, as she opened the door. "What a pleasant surprise." She led the way to the living room.

"What did he want?" Alec cut through the usual formalities

"You weren't spying on me, were you?" She half frowned.

"Of course not. I dropped by to see you and saw Palafox leaving. So what did he want?"

"To be honest, I'm not really sure. At first he said he wanted to pay his respects. He claimed to have known Jeff from the old days. Then he mentioned something about a rumor that someone was trying to make a big deal out of my husband's death and the deaths of some other ex-cops. Of course, I pretended not to know what he was talking about."

"Did he mention my name?"

She shook her head. "He played it very close to the chest and I went along with it."

"I think he was checking you out. Probably talked to Leblanc, the little weasel. By the way, I got a call from Johnson's wife. She sounded scared. The problem is that Johnson doesn't want anybody's help, which means that if she can't convince him to talk to me, well, I don't know what more I can do."

"You think she'll call again?"

"It's hard to say. She said she would. But that was three days ago, so maybe she changed her mind."

"Before I forget, how is your friend Cecil doing?"

"Not good." Alec shook his head. "He's still in a coma. From what I've been told, the longer it lasts, the more likely it is that he's suffered some type of permanent damage."

"I'm sorry to hear that." She paused. "Why don't we continue this in my studio? I've got something to show you." They walked to the other end of the house. "It's a new project. I hope you like it."

Laura entered the room ahead of him. She stepped up to a large painting covered with a white paint-spattered cloth. As if for drama, she reached for the cloth, waited a couple of seconds, and then snatched it away. "So, what do you think?"

Alec crossed his arms and gazed at the painting, a semi-surrealistic rendition of a nude ballerina surrounded by swans. She was dancing as if on water in the middle of a lake filled with lily pods.

"I like it." He nodded. "What do you call it?"

"Take a guess."

Alec shrugged. "I have no idea."

"Oh, honestly, Alec. Take a good look. What do you see? Swans, a lake." She gestured with her hand. "Please don't tell me you've never been to a ballet."

"I hate to disappoint you, but I've never been to one." He shrugged and frowned simultaneously. "What can I say? I'm culturally deficient. So, are you going to tell me?"

"Swan lake," she said, exasperated.

"Of course. I should have known. By Tchaikovsky, right?"

"You redeemed yourself." She smiled. "There's hope for you, yet."

After leaving Laura's house, Alec drove north to Boca Raton to meet his new client, a retired stockbroker from New York. On the phone the night before the man had said only that he had a "delicate problem," the details of which he would prefer to discuss in person.

A maid opened the door. "Please come in. Mr. Spencer had to step out for a moment. He asked if you could wait for him in the den."

"Sure." Alec followed her to the den and sat down on a couch in front of a coffee table made from the trunk of a cypress tree. On top were stacks of old and recent "Sports Illustrated" magazines, including the latest swimsuit edition with a busty blonde on its cover. She wore a wet T-shirt over a skimpy pink bikini.

"May I get you something—a soft drink, a glass of water, anything at all?" said the maid.

Alec smiled politely. "No, thanks. I'll just sit here and wait."

After she had left the room, Alec got up and looked around. He saw an entire wall covered with framed photographs of baseball players, mostly from the fifties and sixties. At least three were of Joe DiMaggio, including a color photo taken during a fundraiser in Palm Beach, shortly before his death.

"Sorry to make you wait, but I had to run out to fill a prescription," said a tall, balding man walking into the room. He reached to shake Alec's hand. "I'm Steve Spencer. Please have a seat. Can I fix you a drink?"

"I'm okay." Alec took a seat.

Mr. Spencer stepped over to a small rattan bar and fixed himself a gin and tonic. "You a sports fan?" He came back and sat across from Alec.

"Off and on I guess, like most guys. I'm more a football fan, though I haven't been to a game in a long time."

Mr. Spencer sipped on his drink. "As you can see, baseball's my game. I used to play when I was in college—had dreams of becoming a pro. Of course, that was before I broke my arm in two places during a freak accident in upstate New York." He put down his drink. "About the delicate problem I mentioned last night, I want you to know I contacted my attorney and told him everything. It was his idea to hire a private investigator."

Alec nodded. "I understand."

Mr. Spencer sighed. "The truth is, I made a mistake—a big one that may wind up costing me my family and my reputation." He reached for his drink and took a quick sip. "A few weeks ago, someone broke into my house and stole something…a DVD. She knew exactly where to look for it. Nothing else was taken."

"She? I'm beginning to see the picture. Has she tried to contact you?"

"Not yet, and that's what worries me. The DVD, as you've probably guessed, contains some pretty explicit activity, if you know what I mean. I recorded it over a year ago—it was an impulse kind of thing—and frankly, I had almost forgotten about it. I stopped seeing her about two months ago."

"So you want me to find her, is that it?"

"Finding her isn't the problem. I know where she lives. What I want you to do is buy back the disk. She may be expecting you." He reached into his pocket, pulled out a piece of paper and handed it to him. "Her name is Donna Wilson; that's her address. She lives with her grandmother in a duplex on the other side of I-95. The best time to catch her would be in the morning. According to my lawyer she hasn't committed a serious crime yet, other than stealing the disk, so you won't be doing anything illegal. It will be a simple transaction between two individuals."

"That's it? What if she refuses to sell it, or claims not to know anything about it? What if she made a copy? They usually do in cases like this."

Mr. Spencer got up to freshen his drink. "I've given the matter a lot of thought. When you tell her how much I'm willing to pay, I'm pretty sure she'll hand it over. After all, that's why she took it, the little cunt. She knew sooner or later I'd come looking for it. As for a possible copy, I'm counting on you to impress upon her that it won't do her any good. I won't pay her another dime. You'll have to make it clear that if she tries to blackmail me I'll go to the police." He sighed. "Let's hope it never comes to that. It would absolutely destroy my relationship with my daughter." He pulled out a thick envelope and dropped it on the table. "Your retainer, plus fifteen thousand dollars. I want you to offer her ten. Give her the whole amount, only—I repeat, only if it's absolutely necessary, understood?"

Alec nodded. "I'll do the best I can." He grabbed the envelope and got up to leave.

"I expect you to do more than your best, Mr. Santana. And to show my appreciation, I'll have a generous bonus waiting for you when you bring back my disk."

He walked Alec to the door. "One more thing. My daughter will be coming in tomorrow for a short visit. She lives in Long Island with her mother. So if you have to call me and I'm not in, just say you're a friend from the club. Any questions?"

Alec shook his head. "Can't think of any. It seems like a straightforward job. I'll call you the moment I have the disk."

CHAPTER 22

*L**ate morning*

Alec double-checked the address, and then pulled into the driveway next to a faded-green Nissan with a dented rear fender and a dangling taillight.

He rang the bell and followed it with a knock.

Seconds later, a young, blondish woman, wearing a pale blue tank top and a pair of cutoffs, answered the door.

"My name is Alec Santana. I wonder if I can speak to you for a moment." He cleared his throat. "Look, I'll cut to the chase. I was hired by someone you know, to retrieve something stolen from him. If you'll give me a moment of your time, I'm sure we can come to an understanding."

"I think you've made a mistake. I don't know what you're talking about." She stepped back to close the door.

"I'm prepared to make you a very generous offer, if you'll give me a chance."

She paused. "I said you've made a mistake. Please go away." She shut the door before Alec could say anything else.

Alec stood there for a couple of seconds, and then turned to leave. He had neared his car when her voice called from behind.

"Maybe we should talk." She held the door open and waited for him to come into the house. They sat at the kitchen table. "I'm not saying I know anything, but suppose I did? I mean, what kind of offer are we talking about?" She moved a coffee cup and a half-eaten Danish to one side.

"Donna. Donna is someone there with you?" said a voice from the bedroom next to the kitchen. "Is it Doctor Kapoor?"

"No Grandma, it's not the doctor, it's just a friend," Donna shouted toward the bedroom. "I'm sorry, you were about to tell me about the offer."

"The deal is this. If you were to return the disk, my client would be willing to pay you up to ten thousand dollars, no questions asked. Lucky you haven't tried to blackmail him, otherwise we probably wouldn't be having this conversation. Listen, I don't know what you were expecting, but it's more than a fair offer. He could have called the cops, you know? And he still may, if you turn down the deal."

Donna crossed her arms. "Any chance you could come back tomorrow after I've had some time to think about it?"

Alec shook his head. "It's a one time offer. If I leave this house without the disk..." He shrugged. "There's no telling what my client will do. It's up to you."

Donna's grandmother moaned. "Donna, I need you. Please bring me my pills." More moaning. "Donna, did you hear me?"

"I'm coming, Grandma," Donna yelled. She stood up. "Give me a moment, Mister...I'm sorry, I forgot your name."

"Santana. Take your time. She doesn't sound good."

Donna stepped up to the counter, picked up a bottle of pills, and then disappeared into the bedroom. A moment later she returned holding the empty bottle.

"That was her last pain pill. Her doctor refuses to give her another prescription unless she visits him at his office, which happens to be on the other side of town. I've tried telling them she's too weak to walk, but they just don't care."

"I'm sorry to hear that. What is wrong with her?"

"Cancer. After ignoring a lump in her breast for a long time, she finally had a mastectomy, but by then it had spread quite a bit. She suffered through chemotherapy and then radiation treatments, which caused some painful burns." She shook her head. "It was horrible. She's still in a great deal of pain. The thing is, they refuse to discuss her case with me because

I'm not her legal guardian." Her lips began to quiver. "I'm sorry, but it makes me angry every time I have to talk about it."

"I don't know what to say." He stood up. "Under the circumstance maybe I should come back later."

"What did he tell you about me?"

"My client? He told me what I needed to know, which wasn't very much. And I didn't ask any questions—it wasn't any of my business. No offense, but it was just another job which seemed too good to turn down."

"I'm not a prostitute, you know." She said it as though making a proclamation.

"I never thought you were, not that it matters."

"Well, it matters to me." She slapped her hand on her chest. "You come in here expecting me to roll over and give you the disk. Well, it's not going to happen. Not until you hear me out." She shook her head. "Oh, what's the use. You probably wouldn't believe me anyway."

Alec stared at her for a moment. "I'm a pretty good listener, especially over a cup of coffee."

A long silence. "You're not at all what I expected," she said, her lips forming a faint smile. "I figured whoever he hired to do his dirty work would be more of an asshole." She poured coffee into two cups, and then brought them over to the table and sat down. "You really want to know how it happened, I mean, how it all started?"

"Sure," Alec nodded, "if you really want to tell me."

Donna took a sip of her coffee. "I met him at a bar where I used to hang out on weekends. That was before my grandmother got really sick. She raised me since I was twelve, but that's another story. Anyway, one night Mr. Spencer offered to buy me a drink. It was no big thing. The guy looked lonely and he seemed like a nice enough fellow. Well, I saw him a few times after that and one night I mentioned I was looking for a job, any job 'cause I had no skills."

"I'm beginning to understand." Alec stirred his coffee.

"When he told me that he might know of a job, I said 'great, tell me all about it.' By that time, I'd been out of work for almost three months and the bills were piling up. Of course, my grandmother was getting sicker by the day." She sighed. "I should've known it was too good to be true—there really was no job, at least not the kind I imagined. One night as I was leaving the bar, he followed me to my car and told me what he had in mind. He wanted…oral sex. He waved a hundred-dollar bill in my face. I went for it without even thinking. We did it in the back seat of my car, right there in the parking lot."

"After that, I was hooked, so to speak." She looked down, a little embarrassed. "He'd call me almost every week and I'd drive over to his house in Boca Raton, usually on the maid's day off. He raised it to two hundred bucks for each visit." She shrugged. "I needed the money, what can I say? Then when my grandma got really sick, I asked if he could front me some money—just a couple of grand to help pay expenses—but he wouldn't even consider it. To him I was just a whore who was good for only one thing. I got so angry that I stormed out of the house and never went back. Afterward, I remembered the DVD and I suddenly got an idea."

"To blackmail him?"

She shook her head. "I thought about it, but to be honest I had no real plan. I knew if I had the disk, he'd come looking for it sooner or later. All I wanted was an advance, for God's sake, and he acted like I was trying to rob him or something. The fact is, I was desperate." Her voice began to break. "She's going fast, and without anyone to help me, I don't know what I'm going to do."

They heard moans coming from the bedroom.

"Excuse me, but I have to check on Grandma." Donna stood up. "But before I do, let me give you what you came for." She reached underneath the sink, pulled out the disk from inside a plastic bag and handed it to Alec. "In case you're wondering, I didn't make a copy."

Alec hesitated for a second, and then pulled out a thick envelope containing the money. "There's fifteen thousand in there." He dropped it on the table. "For what it's worth, I think you've earned it. By the way, you may want to inquire about hospice. It shouldn't cost you anything and they'll help you with your grandmother's care." He pulled out his business card and left it on the table.

Donna attempted a smile. "Thanks…for everything."

"I'll see my way out." He stood to leave. "Good luck, and don't forget what I said about hospice." He could hear the old woman's moans, even as he closed the door.

From his car, he picked up his phone and dialed Spencer's number. He let it ring six times. No answer. A minute later, he got a call back.

"How did it go?" Mr. Spencer said.

"Just like you said. All she wanted was the money. She drove a hard bargain and I had to give her the full fifteen."

"The fucking bitch. I hope she chokes on it, she and her white trash grandmother."

"I'll be there in twenty minutes."

Mr. Spencer opened the door and led the way to the den. "Before we conclude our arrangement, let's check it out," he said, his tone businesslike. "I want to make sure it's the right disk. For fifteen thousand bucks, it better be. My daughter is away shopping and the maid won't bother us, she's in the other side of the house." He slid the disk into the player and stood back.

They watched as a giggling Donna stripped naked while Mr. Spencer lay on the bed, fully clothed. He had a dumb look on his face as he unzipped his pants.

Alec felt uncomfortable and backed away. He waited for Mr. Spencer to turn off the player. But the man seemed to be enjoying it and let it run to the end.

"Good work, Mr. Santana," Mr. Spencer said, finally. He reached into an envelope, pulled out a check and slipped it into Alec's shirt pocket.

Alec started for the door. "I've got another appointment. If you need me, you've got my number."

Returning to his apartment, the first thing Alec did was check his voice mail. He played them back while he went to the kitchen, grabbed a beer and plopped down on the couch. He sat up when he heard the fifth message.

"I'm sorry I didn't get back to you sooner, Mr. Santana but my husband is always around. He's been talking to someone in Miami—I don't know who—trying to get some fake documents so we can leave the country. It's a crazy idea and I told him so, but he refuses to listen. We're staying at the Siesta Motel, room 245, near Lake Wales off Highway 27. I don't know how long we'll be here so please hurry. I'm sure he'll listen to you once he knows he can trust you."

"Yes!" Alec shouted. He took a swig of his beer. After a moment, he picked up the phone and dialed Laura's number.

"She finally called," Alec said, eager to share the good news. "When I got in a little while ago, there was a message from her on my recorder."

"What are you talking about?"

"Johnson's wife. They're staying at a place near Lake Wales...the Siesta motel off Highway 27. I'm driving up there first thing in the morning."

"She must really be desperate. What if Johnson refuses to talk to you? What if—"

"I can't worry about that. The main thing is that I'll finally get a chance to see him. Once I'm there, I'm sure he'll come around. I mean, what choice does he have? It's either me or Victor."

"When you put it that way, I guess you're right." She paused. "Good luck. I have a feeling you're going to need it."

"Thanks, I'll call when I get back."

CHAPTER 23

The motel wasn't hard to find—a cluster of small, fifties-style cottages with a large roadside sign in the shape of a Mexican sombrero. He drove through the parking lot, spotted 245 and pulled into the closest slot. A moment later, a young couple with a baby came out of the room.

According to the manager, a middle-aged man with a north Florida accent, Johnson and his wife had checked out in the middle of the night.

"Damn it," Alec said, under his breath. "Did they give any indication where they were going?"

The manager shook his head. "They seemed to be in hurry, at least the man did. She stayed in the car, while he came in and paid the bill."

Alec frowned. "Thanks." He turned to leave.

"Wait a minute. I just thought of something." The man opened a drawer and reached for an envelope. "Your name wouldn't happen to be Alec Santana, would it?"

"Yes." Alec nodded.

"The maid found this under the bed." He handed him an envelope with Alec's name scribbled on it.

Alec tore it open and read the note.

My husband thought someone was out there, watching us from the parking lot. He got scared and insisted we had to move to a safer place, to a small cabin deep in the woods. If you found the note, wait until I call you at the phone in the manager's office at exactly 12:15 p.m.

Alec slipped the note back in the envelope and looked at his watch. "Listen. I know this sounds crazy, but you may be getting a call around noon... someone wanting talk to me. I'll be back in a couple of hours."

The man shrugged. "I ain't going nowhere."

Alec left the motel, drove around the area, stopped for gas, and then made it back at 11:45 a.m.

He grabbed the morning newspaper and took a seat in a wicker chair next to a vending machine.

"It must sure be important...this call you're waiting for," the man said.

"It is. If you don't mind I'll just sit here and wait."

"No problem." He turned around to finish doing some filing.

A few minutes later, at almost 12:15 p.m. the phone rang. Alec jumped to his feet.

The man nodded. "Yes, m'am I understand." He picked up a pen and wrote. "Can you please spell it?" Short pause. "Parrinello. Ursula Parrinello. I'll put you down for three nights."

Alec sighed and sat back down. He waited another twenty minutes, and then stood to leave. "I guess she's not going to call," he said, disappointed. "Can you do me a favor? If she calls, can you give her this number?" He wrote his cell number on a piece of paper.

The phone rang.

"Yes, he's right here," the man said into the receiver. "One second." He reached over to hand the phone to Alec.

"Hello?" Alec pulled out a pen and a three by five card.

"Listen carefully," Mrs. Johnson said. "We're staying at a small cabin in the woods just south of Ocala. Take I-75; you'll come to a road that intersects the highway near a large Chevron sign. Make a right turn and you'll be on a long, winding road that splits into two dirt roads, one to the left, one to the right. Take the left road for about three miles until you get to a faded NO TRESPASSING sign. Turn there and the cabin is about a hundred yards behind a row of tall pine trees."

"I'm on my way." Alec handed the phone back to the manager. "Thanks."

On the way out, he picked up a map and hurried to his car.

Alec made good time. When he saw the faded NO TRESPASSING sign, he slowed and turned into a long, semi-graveled driveway. He pulled over near a row of tall pine trees, glanced around, and then walked up to the cabin, which looked gray and neglected: fallen shingles, windows boarded up, except for the front one facing a yard filled with broken tree limbs and scattered leaves and debris.

"You have no business here," an angry voice said from inside. "Leave us alone."

"I came a long way to see you, Mr. Johnson. I know why you're running and I think I can help. Please open the door."

"I've got a loaded gun. I swear to God I'll shoot you if you try to come in here," Johnson shouted. "You hear me? Just turn around and go back where you came from."

Alec heard Mrs. Johnson arguing with her husband. "The man is only trying to help us. Just give him a chance. If you don't open the door right now, I'm leaving and I mean for good. Now put down that gun before you hurt someone."

After a brief silence Johnson opened the door. "Come on in." Not quite six-feet-tall with a stocky build, he wore his belt below his waistline, which caused his large belly to extend outward.

Alec stepped inside and followed him to a seating area in front of the window.

"Let's get one thing straight," Johnson said. "I don't trust you and neither did Donahue. If you'd left him alone, like he asked, he'd probably still be alive."

"Now hold on there." Alec raised his hand. "You know very well my wanting to talk to him had nothing to with his death. The fact is he knew too much, or at least someone thought he did. The papers said it was an accident, but you and I know different, don't we?"

Johnson looked at Alec, and then at his wife, who sat next to him. "Before we go any further, tell me how much you know. If I think you're being straight with me, I'll do the same."

"Fair enough." Alec shifted his body, and then related his conversations with Ben's widow and the widows of the other ex-cops who had killed themselves. "At first I just wanted to help Julie who wanted to know why Ben had killed himself for no reason at all, at least none she was aware of. But when I found out about the money…"

"Then you know about the letters," Johnson interrupted.

Alec nodded. "When I saw what it was all about: Victor, the money in the house…it all made sense, except for Ben's participation. I'd known Ben for over twenty years and I knew he couldn't have been involved." He looked away for second. "There just had to be some logical explanation."

"Tell him, Rudy, tell him the truth," said his wife. "You said you'd level with him."

Johnson looked at her, and then turned to Alec. "I'm still not sure if I can trust you," he said, a scowl forming across his face. "Do I have your word you won't go to the cops, no matter what I say?"

Alec hesitated. "Sure. You have my word, if that's the way you want it. I'll try to keep an open mind."

"Okay then, here's what really happened." He took a deep breath. "To begin with, you were right. Ben was no thief. The night of the fire, he got there right after we found the money. He never knew anything about it. We had already decided to keep it and figured Ben wouldn't go along with what we had in mind."

"I knew it," Alec said, with restrained excitement.

Johnson continued. "You have to remember that the guy who died in the fire was probably a drug dealer. It was dirty money. It's not like we were stealing it. Anyway, the next day, the four of us: me, Mendoza, Conway and Harrison, met to discuss what we were going to do with it—two million bucks. Harrison wanted to split it up four ways right then and there, but Mendoza pointed out it would look too suspicious. We could never explain our new found wealth, not on an average cop's salary." He turned to his wife. "Why don't you bring us some whiskey? I suddenly need a drink."

Mrs. Johnson got up, went to the kitchen and came back with a bottle of Wild Turkey and two glasses. She set them on the coffee table.

Johnson poured a little under two fingers into each glass. He reached for one and took a quick gulp. "Getting back to the money. After a lot of arguing, we finally came up with a plan. We'd wait fifteen years before splitting it up. It was to be our nest egg for when we retired." He sighed. "The truth is we were scared. We didn't want to make the same mistake other cops had made in similar situations, which was to split the money too soon and wind up in jail."

"What did you do with the money?"

"I was getting to that." Johnson took another gulp of whiskey. "We put it in a safe and buried it in a field near the everglades. We agreed that from that point on, we'd have minimal contact with each other until the fifteen years had passed. This coming December would be the fifteenth year."

"What if somebody tried to get to it sooner? I'm sure you considered the possibility."

"Of course, we did. That's why we decided to have only one guy bury the money, so only he would know where it was. The most obvious guy was Conway. We figured he would be the least tempted to want to spend it. He had already married a rich lady, so it's not like he needed more money."

"Tell him the rest," his wife prodded.

Johnson nodded. "When Mendoza got the letter—he was the first to get one—he freaked out and called everyone involved. Then, one by one, we got the same letter. It didn't make any sense that after all these years, Victor, the kid we saved, was blaming us for allowing his parents to die. We felt trapped, and we sure as hell couldn't go to the police. Then, when he sent us a copy of a newspaper article about a fatal accident on the expressway, we knew we were up against a fucking psycho."

"What article?"

"About Harrison's widow. Someone had run her car off the road, causing it to slam into the retaining wall. She died on the way to hospital." He got up, stepped across the room and retrieved a small piece of paper. "This was clipped to the article that each of us received."

Alec read the note:

Take this as a warning. The same thing will happen to your loved ones if you do not comply with my demands. Their lives are in your hands. If you ignore me, I swear, on the graves of my parents, that I will arrange for another 'accident'.

Alec put down the note. "This is incredible. It must have been sheer agony for Ben. To be honest I don't know what I would've done had I been in his place." He looked away for a second, then reached for his whiskey and took a big gulp.

"So now you know as much I do," Johnson said, his tone calm. "Unlike the others I wasn't ready to give in to him, not that the thought didn't cross my mind." He looked at his wife. "I wanted to spare her from all of this, from having to know the whole ugly story. But I had no choice and I told her all about it. We stayed holed up in the house for days, afraid to even go to the grocery store."

"What about the money? Did Conway ever tell anybody where he buried it?"

"To tell you the truth, that was the last thing on our minds. Then, when I heard he'd killed himself, I knew we'd never see it again." He sighed. "Maybe it was just as well."

"You sure he didn't tell anybody? It just seems hard to believe he wouldn't have told at least one other person. People seldom take that kind of secret to the grave, unless they have no choice or no one to trust."

Johnson thought about it for a moment. "I really can't think of anyone. We purposely stayed away from each other all these years, so it's anybody's guess who he might have told."

Alec crossed his arms, and then scratched the side of his face. "Ever heard the name Rosario? In a letter Ben wrote to his wife just before he killed himself he said he wanted me to know that Rosario held all the answers. It was like he had a suspicion of some kind, but he wasn't really sure."

Johnson shook his head. "Never heard of her."

"She may have something to do with Victor. But at this point it's pure speculation. Anyway, I've asked around but nobody seems to know anything about her. I'm not giving up, though. I have a feeling that if and when I find her, Victor won't be far away."

"So what's your plan, now that I've told you everything?" Johnson asked. "You said you could help us."

"Well, to start with, I think you should stay here, at least for the next couple of days. Meanwhile I'll work on trying to find a safer place, maybe out of the state in North Georgia. I have an old college buddy who used to work for the Secret Service. He runs an exclusive bed and breakfast place on the Georgia-Carolina border. I know I can count on him to help us out. Maybe I can get you in there under a bogus name. By the way, we have to assume Victor did not come alone. I don't mean to scare you but he or one his men tried to run me and my friend off the road as we were driving out to the everglades. I wasn't badly hurt, but my friend is still in a coma."

"I don't feel safe here," Mrs. Johnson said, "I don't know why. Maybe because we're too isolated. Can't you get us out of here any sooner?" She reached for a cigarette and took a quick drag.

"I'll try," Alec said. "I'll tell you what. Just give me twenty-four hours and I promise I'll—"

Suddenly, a gunshot rang out. It was followed by a thud as a bullet smashed through the window. It whizzed past Alec's ear and struck a wall to his left. It missed Mrs. Johnson by inches.

"Get down, get down!" Alec shouted.

"Oh my God, they found us." Mrs. Johnson crouched as low as she could. "What are we going to do?"

"Stay calm, stay low," Alec said. "It came from behind the pine trees." He turned to Johnson. "Where's your gun?"

"Over there, on the kitchen table." Johnson pointed. He lay sideways on the floor, facing his wife.

"Go get it," Alec said. "Meanwhile I'll slip out the back and see if I can go around, maybe catch him by surprise." He crawled toward the door, opened it slowly and stuck his head out. He saw, heard nothing, then made a dash toward a tree in the middle of the yard and took cover. From there he ran toward the woods, circled all around and paused when he came within a few yards from where the shot had been fired. He waited, listened, and then heard twigs breaking: someone running through the brush. He ran after him, gun in hand, and stopped when he couldn't tell which way the man had turned.

He stood still, silence all around.

Suddenly came a kaboom, kaboom—familiar sounds of a shotgun firing—coming from the cabin. He bolted toward the wooden structure, stopped outside the door, and then stormed into the front room.

"No, no," he uttered seeing the bloodied, torn up bodies of Johnson and his wife on the floor. It had been quick and brutal: bits of flesh and brain matter splattered all around them.

Alec began to hyperventilate. He went to the back—the door was still open—looked around, and then closed it. He checked the front, locked the door and waited. Were they still out there? How many were there? At least two, he figured. He moved the sofa to one side and crouched behind it. A poor shield, but it would have to do. His .38 was no match for a shotgun, and the only thing he hoped for was that he'd have a chance to get the first round off, maybe knock the shooter off his feet.

Seconds later a siren wailed in the distance. It got louder as it neared the cabin, and then louder still as a sheriff's cruiser pulled into the yard. They were responding to a frantic call from Mrs. Johnson, he later found out.

Alec breathed a long sigh of relief. Still shaken, he stepped out of the cabin with his hands in the air and explained what happened.

Hours later, and after much questioning, he left the scene. He drove all through the night and arrived in Miami around one in the morning.

CHAPTER 24

Mid afternoon

A recent downpour had left the air feeling hot and steamy. "Need some help?" Alec strolled into Julie's yard.

She was tending her garden of herbs and green peppers. "Alec, what a surprise," she said, from under a large straw hat. She wore cutoffs and one of her husband's old, white dress shirts. "I hadn't heard from you in a while. Everything okay?"

He looked at her for a long moment. "I have a confession to make. I continued to work on Ben's suicide after you asked me not to. I wasn't going to say anything, not until I found out why he felt that he had no choice."

"For God's sake, what is it? If you found something, I have a right to know."

"Let's sit down." They walked over to a picnic table in the middle of the yard.

"Look Alec, I'm much stronger now, so don't feel like you have to hold back. I want to know everything, and I mean everything."

He took a deep breath. "It wasn't easy…having to learn what Ben must have gone through. Remember the torn letter, the one I picked up near where Ben's car was found? Well, my friend Cecil worked on it, like a puzzle. Turned out, it was a message from Victor, the boy they saved that night. He blamed Ben and the others for letting his parents die in the fire."

"But why? Why would he blame them? It doesn't make sense."

"Because of the money," Alec blurted out. "Victor figured that the so-called heroes had stolen two million dollars from a suitcase in the attic. He claimed they were more interested in stealing the money than saving his parents."

Julie gasped. "Oh, my God, is it true? Please don't tell me Ben was involved."

Alec reached over and placed his hand over hers. "I never believed he was, not even for a minute." He took his time repeating everything Johnson had said, including that Ben had arrived later and had no part in stealing the money. He told her about the note and the copy of the newspaper article Ben and the others had received. When he was through, he said, "The truth is, I may have done more harm than good by going up to see him. They were counting on me to help them, and I let them down."

Julie's eyes filled with tears. "I don't know what to say. Ben killed himself to protect me and I knew nothing about it." She shook her head. "It doesn't make any sense. Why didn't he tell me? I would have understood and we could have done something about it." She sniffled and brushed away her tears.

Alec nodded. "I just wish I could've done more for the Johnsons. I told the cops about Victor and all the rest, but I'm not so sure they believed me. If they call Detective Palafox they'll probably get a different version. He'll downplay everything so he won't have to get involved."

"Just like he did with Ben's suicide."

"That's right. It could very well mean that their killers may never have to pay for what they did."

"What about the money? You think it's still buried somewhere?"

He considered it for a second. "I don't know. From the very beginning, I thought it strange that Victor never asked for the return of the money, not even a portion of it. He made it clear the motive behind the letters was revenge, pure and simple. But now, I'm beginning to wonder. I can't help but think—"

His phone rang; he answered it on the second ring.

"It's a miracle," Kathy said. "I was sitting by his bed reading to him from an old Hemingway novel when all of a sudden his head moved. Then he opened his eyes and stared at me, as though he didn't know who I was. I said 'Cecil, can you hear me? Do you know who I am?' The next moment he said he was hungry and wanted me to get him some breakfast…a stack of blueberry pancakes, his absolute favorite."

"Thank God. I knew he would snap out of it, I just knew it. So, when can I see him?"

"Anytime. The doctor says it'll do him some good to see familiar faces."

"Say no more, I'll be there as soon as I can. Don't tell him I'm coming. I want to surprise him."

Alec pressed the Off key. "That was Cecil's wife. He just came out of the coma. The doctors had practically given up on him. Look, I need to go to the hospital, to see how he's doing. Will you be okay?"

She attempted a smile. "Go see your friend. I'll be all right." She got up and kissed him on the cheek.

When Alec entered Cecil's room, he paused and waited for Kathy to finish combing his hair, which had grown long and unruly, especially over the ears. "That's enough." He grinned. "You don't want him to look too good. I hear this place is full of pretty nurses just dying to put the make on a handsome guy like Cecil."

Kathy laughed, and so did Cecil who was having difficulty focusing.

Alec stepped closer. "You sure had us worried, ole buddy. Welcome back. So, how do you feel?"

Cecil seemed a bit groggy. "Like I just been kicked in the head by a mule."

"The doctors say he'll continue feeling some discomfort for the next few days," Kathy said. "After that he should be just fine."

Cecil nodded. "I can't wait to get the hell out of here. I have a lot of catching up to do. Anything new on the case?"

A burly young man pushing a wheelchair appeared. "He's scheduled for an EEG. It shouldn't take long."

Alec stepped back and watched as the young man helped Cecil into the chair. He stayed to chat with Kathy, and then left the room ten minutes later.

After leaving the hospital, he called Laura; they agreed to meet at a coffee shop on U.S 1, near the Fort Lauderdale airport.

"I meant to call you earlier." Alec stirred his coffee. "But I was too bummed out from everything that happened." He filled her in on his meeting with the Johnsons and the brutal way they were killed. When he was through, he took a deep breath and shook his head. "In a way I feel partly responsible. I was supposed to protect them and there was nothing I could do. Hell, I thought they were going to finish me off, and they might have if the cops hadn't shown up. Mrs. Johnson called them at the last minute, thank God."

Laura's eyes widened. "That's absolutely incredible. I would've been scared witless. Did you see who they were? What about the cops, couldn't they catch them?"

Alec shook his head. "I saw nothing, absolutely nothing. Couldn't even tell you how many were involved, though I think there were two, at least. As for the cops, there wasn't much they could do. They had no descriptions, no car to put a BOLO on, not even a helpful neighbor who might've seen or heard something. It's going to be a tough one to work, I can tell you that."

"Didn't you tell them the reason they killed Johnson?"

"Of course, but I think it went over their heads. They thought it was too bizarre. Four dead ex-cops, a mystery man called Victor, two million dollars no one has seen. It was information overload. And don't forget, they'll probably want to talk to Palafox, the useless piece of turd. Knowing him, he'll put cold water on everything I told them."

"Which means Victor and his friends will get away with murder." She frowned.

"That's right." He reached for his cup to take a sip, and then set it back down. "Let me ask you something. Did Jeff ever mention anything about the money? I don't mean directly, but maybe in a casual kind of way. I guess I'm still bothered by the fact that no one besides Jeff knew where it was hidden."

"Like I told you before, Jeff and I were barely speaking to each other. I would've been the last person he'd confide in. If you ask me, the only reason Jeff went along with the plan in the first place was because he wanted something to fall back on, in case we ever split up, which would've happened if he hadn't killed himself. We had a pre-nup that made sure he'd get only what he brought into the marriage, which wasn't much."

"Interesting." Alec sipped his coffee.

"Well, at least you found out your friend was one of the good guys, after all. Isn't that enough?"

He hesitated. "I don't know how to answer that. I mean, sure I'm glad I was able to clear Ben's name. It meant a lot to his widow. On the other hand, I have this lingering feeling it's not really over."

"What do you mean?"

"Rosario. I still can't get her out of my mind. Who is she? What does she have to do with all of this?"

Laura sighed. "Look, Alec, take my advice. Let the cops take if from here. If they find Victor or if they don't, it's not going to change anything. You're a P.I. now and you should be thinking about building up your business. In fact, whenever you say the word, I'll call a few friends, some with pretty deep pockets, and let them know you're available."

Alec thought about it for a long moment. "You know what? I think you're right. Tomorrow I'm going to start looking for an office, nothing fancy, mind you, just something big enough for a desk and a filing cabinet. So go ahead, tell your friends, especially the ones with deep pockets. I might as well start at the top, right?"

"Great, I'll get on it right away." She got up from the table. "I hate to run, but I've got a doctor's appointment on the other side of town."

"Oh, I almost forgot. Cecil is out of his coma and it looks like he's going to be okay. I just left him, but I didn't get a chance to talk to him that much. I'll see him again in a day or two when he's fully recovered."

"That's fantastic. I was really rooting for him. I'd like to meet him someday. Call me when you've moved into your office."

He waved to her and stayed to finish his coffee and the rest of a piece of key lime pie they were sharing.

CHAPTER 25

"I got here as fast as I could," Alec said. "What happened?" He was distracted by a stream of somber-faced detectives and crime scene technicians entering Sharon Halverson's ground-level apartment.

"We were responding to a disturbance call from one of the neighbors," Bonnie said. "Unfortunately, we got here too late. She'd been stabbed multiple times in the upper chest and neck area. By the look of the cuts on her hands and forearms, she must've put up a helluva struggle. There was no forced entry, so we figure it must've been someone she knew, maybe a john. According to the guy who lived next door, she was hooking from out of her apartment. Probably didn't want to leave her baby alone."

"Are you sure it's her?"

Bonnie nodded. "She looks like the girl in your picture: about the same age, same general features. She had I.D. under a couple of names, including Sharon Halverson. Of course, we'll know for sure when we run her prints."

Alec paused. "I don't know how I'm going to break it to her mother, her natural mother, that is. Have you notified her adopted family?"

"They're doing that right now." She shook her head. "What a shame, a pretty girl like that."

They heard a baby crying and turned toward the open doorway.

"Is that Sharon's baby?" Alec asked.

Bonnie nodded. "A beautiful baby girl. They're coming out now."

A female deputy carried the infant to a waiting car, which sped away quickly.

"So what's going to happen to her?"

"They'll take her to the hospital, to make sure she's okay, and then Child Protective Services will probably allow a family member to claim her. Of course, if no one comes forward, for whatever reason, they'll put her up for adoption."

Alec stroked his chin. "Do me a favor. Can you keep me posted?"

"Sure, I'll be glad to. Look, I've got to go back in there. I just wanted to make sure you had the full story."

"Thanks, I appreciate it. And good luck. I think you're going to need it."

Back in his car, Alec dialed Irene Bailey's number. He let it ring five times and hung up. It was almost a relief she didn't answer. He wouldn't have known how to break it to her.

Later, as he drove back to his place, his phone rang.

"I recognized your phone number on my caller I.D.," Irene said. "Did you find her? Is that why you called?"

Alec pulled over to the side of the road. "I called you because…maybe it's best if I tell you in person. I can be there in twenty minutes."

"Tell me what? She doesn't want to meet me, is that it?"

"I never thought I'd have to say this." Alec hesitated. "But your daughter was murdered. I'm sorry, I'm really sorry."

"Murdered? Oh, my God. It can't be." She started to cry. "I never even got a chance to hold her, to tell her why I had to give her up. It's not fair, it's not fair."

"I know. Unfortunately, I wasn't able to find her in time. If I had, it might've made a difference."

"How did it happen?" she asked after a long silence.

"She was found stabbed in her apartment. You'll probably hear all about it on the evening news. The cops are still on the scene. We won't know what really happened until they conduct an investigation, which may take some time." Brief pause. "There's something you should know. Sharon had a baby girl. She was in the apartment when it happened."

"Is she all right?"

"She's fine. She's being taken to the hospital for a checkup. Then Child Protective Services will eventually turn her over to someone in the family, the mother, I suppose."

Irene let out a sigh. "So that's it, then. After all these years, not knowing where she was, how she was doing…" She started to cry again. "I feel like I've lost her twice. She was my baby and now she's with the angels." She sniffled. "I'm sorry but I have to hang up. Goodbye Mr. Santana."

Alec dropped the phone and sat there for a long moment. If he had found her sooner, he could have saved her. That was all he could think of.

Back home and hours later, Alec got an unexpected call from Sergeant Carter, one of the deputies he'd met at the cabin where the Johnsons were killed.

"I'm surprised to hear from you," Alec said. "How's the case going?"

"Well, up until this afternoon, we were still arguing amongst ourselves, whether or not to put any stock on this wild suicide theory of yours. Then about an hour ago, we got this anonymous phone call from a man with a south Georgia accent. He claimed he knew who the shooters were. He said they were a couple of good ole boys, Lester and Harold Jackson from South Carolina. Supposedly, Johnson had sold them a quantity of cocaine that turned out to be mostly talcum powder, and so they had come back to settle the score, Dixie style. He gave a brief description of the two, including the car they were driving. Then he hung up as though afraid we might trace his number."

"Do you believe him?"

"At this point, I have no reason not to. Besides, we all think it makes a whole lot more sense than your crazy suicide and vengeance theory."

"You're not going to rule it out are you?" Alec said, a tinge of concern in his voice.

"Only until we run out of leads, which brings me to my question and the reason I called. I want you to level with me, you knowing as much about Johnson as anybody. Did you know he was a drug dealer?"

"Is that a question or an assumption?"

"You know what I mean," the deputy fired back. "I just want to know if you uncovered anything, even a rumor, that Johnson might have been involved in drugs, selling, buying or whatever."

"Look, as far I know, Johnson was just an ordinary guy. He was a Mason, for God's sake. I may be wrong, but he just didn't fit the profile."

"Well, I respect your opinion, you being a former cop, but we still have to check it out. Oh, before I forget, I talked to Detective Palafox from Miami. I probably shouldn't be telling you this, but he suggested we disregard your story. Claimed it was all speculation based on very old information."

Alec could feel his jaw muscles tighten. "Yeah, well, I'm not surprised. Thanks for letting me know."

He fumed as he hung up the phone. "That fucking son-of-a- bitch. He did it again."

CHAPTER 26

The next morning, Alec dropped by the hospital to check on Cecil. The first thing he noticed was that someone had cut his hair. He looked rested, more alert and quickly sat up, eager to chat.

"Boy, am I glad to see you," Cecil said, "I'm going stir crazy. They won't even let me get out of bed, except to go to the john." His speech was much improved, with almost no hesitation.

"Well, I see I don't have to ask how you're feeling. So when are they releasing you?"

"The doctor is coming by to see me later today. If everything checks out okay, I should be out this afternoon. Why don't you grab a chair and sit down? I hope you're not in a hurry because I have a lot of questions. The last thing I remember we were in the car, skidding out of control, and then the next moment everything went totally black. Did the cops catch the guy in the truck?"

Alec shook his head and pulled up a chair. "He was long gone by the time the cops arrived. It was me they were after, you know. You just happened to be in the same car and I'm sorry for that."

"Thanks for letting me know. Next time I'll make sure we go in separate cars." He chuckled. "You really think he was trying to kill you?"

"He probably just wanted to scare me, which I have to admit, he succeeded in doing. My guess is that it was a warning to get off the case, or else. Well, they won't have to worry about me anymore. It's over, I'm off the case."

"You don't mean that, do you?"

Alec looked away for a moment, and then related everything that had happened, from the day of the accident to his meeting with the Johnsons and its aftermath in the cabin in north Florida. When he was through, he leaned back and shook his head. "I let them down." His voice dropped to almost a whisper. "They were counting on me to protect them and I let them down."

"Hey, it wasn't your fault. Seems to me that whoever did it was already on to him and they would have found him whether or not you showed up." He crossed his hands behind his back. "What about the drug angle...you think Johnson was a doper?"

Alec took a moment to answer. "To be honest, I'm not really sure. But I'll tell you this, Johnson was afraid of one person and only one person: Victor. So, when the deputy mentioned a possible drug connection, my first reaction was that someone deliberately steered the investigation in the wrong direction. It's the oldest trick in the book. Make an anonymous phone call and provide just enough facts and then hang up before they can ask any questions."

"I see what you mean."

"Well, like I said before, I'm off the case, so it's pointless to speculate about this or that. Though I have to admit, I still have this lingering feeling that it's not really over. There are too many loose ends that were never resolved."

"Like Rosario?"

Alec nodded "Exactly. Then there's the money. Almost fifteen years later, and it's nowhere to be found. There are other things too, like the fact they never found Conway's body, which never set right with me."

"You don't think he might still be alive, do you? It doesn't make sense. Unless...unless he recovered the money and disappeared, maybe in some other country. But why? He had it all, a rich beautiful wife, a house on the water." He shrugged. "I just don't get it."

"When I first met Laura, one of the things she said was that prior to the suicide, she was already planning to divorce him. Then just yesterday, she told me about their pre-nup agreement that would have left him practically broke. Anyway it's just another piece of the puzzle that never quite fit."

"What about Victor?"

"What about him? He got what he wanted. My guess is he's probably back in Argentina." He stood up. "Well, we can speculate forever but it isn't going to change a thing. Besides, I've got some things to do, like finding an office for my P.I. business, getting a client or two and," he smiled, "making sure I've got a sweet, hard body lying next to me at least once a week."

Cecil laughed. "What about Laura? I figured you two would be more than friends by now. A merry widow. A rich one to boot. Not a bad combination."

Alec ran his fingers through his hair. "I have to admit that when I first met her, I was really attracted to her. She was a classy lady, like no one I'd ever met before. But then when I got to know her…I knew it couldn't work out for us. It's hard to explain. We're still friends, though. She even promised to send me a client or two."

Cecil hesitated. "If you ever decide to take on a partner, can you let me know? Not now, but in the future when your business picks up, which I know it will."

"You're not serious are you? You'd be giving up part of your pension."

"There's more to life than just a pension. Look, I think you'll agree that you and I made a pretty good team with Ben's case. And we can do it again—you doing field work and me doing research. An unbeatable combo, I'd say."

Alec considered it for a moment. "You know what? I think you're right. We would make a good team. Let's think about it some more and in a few months if you still feel the same, well, we can make it official."

Cecil sat up and extended his hand. "Put it there *partner*," he said grinning.

Alec shook his hand and stayed to chat for a few minutes longer.

He spent the rest of the day looking for office space. After checking out half a dozen locations from Fort Lauderdale to Miami, he settled on a two-room office in a grayish, nondescript building off West Dixie Highway in North Miami Beach.

On his way home he got a call from Laura, about a potential client.

"When you said you'd try to send me cases, I didn't think it would be this soon. What do you have?"

"Why don't you come over and I'll give you all the details? By the way, the person I spoke to said money was no object."

"Say no more, I'll be there in half an hour."

When he got there, the door was open and he called out to her. "Laura. Hello, anybody home?"

"Just come on in," Laura said from the kitchen. "Make yourself at home. I'll be right there."

Alec stepped inside and sat down on the couch in the living room.

A moment later, she appeared with an open bottle of Dom Pérignon and two goblets. She poured a little into each glass and sat next to him.

"To celebrate your new client." She lifted her glass.

Alec picked up his goblet and brought it up to hers. He took a quick sip and set it back down. "You really didn't have to do this." He smiled. "Are you trying to spoil me or something?"

"Or something," she said with a sly grin. "I just thought it'd be nice to mark the occasion. We might even make it a tradition each time you start a big case. What do you think?"

Alec laughed. "Okay by me. Only next time, I'll pick the booze." He took another sip of champagne. "So tell me about the client. Is it someone you know?"

"Actually I've never met her, but I've talked to her on the phone. She's a friend of a friend of mine. Has a mansion on Miami Beach and is well known in the arts community. She donates heavily to the ballet and other dance groups. Her pet project for the past couple of years has been a new dance company called Flamenco del Sol. The case has something to do with one of the dancers. According to my friend, someone has been stalking the girl for the past few weeks and the cops have apparently done little or nothing about it."

"I'm not sure I understand. If all they want is a bodyguard—"

"Look, I don't have all the details, but my understanding is that they want you to investigate the matter. I told them you were the best P. I. in town and that you'd just finished working a big case for me, which is true in a way. If everything turns out well, I'm sure your name will soon be on every socialite's Rolodex from here to Palm Beach. And that, as they say in Hollywood, is like money in the bank."

Alec took a long sip of champagne. "Like money in the bank. I like the sound of that. So when can I meet this new client that's supposed to put me on the fast track?"

Laura handed him a piece of paper with the client's name and phone number. "They're having a dress rehearsal tomorrow at the Colony Theater around ten in the morning, so you may want to see her there."

"Thanks, I think I'll do that." He downed the last of his champagne and got up to leave.

"What's the hurry?" She refilled his glass. "This is supposed to be a celebration, remember? Besides, it's beginning to rain, part of a squall that's coming in from the ocean. Why don't you wait until it passes?"

Alec ambled across the room and looked out the window. Dark, ominous-looking clouds were moving inland; the intermittent sounds of thunder echoed from miles away. Suddenly the wind picked up, sending debris and fallen palm fronds flying across the yard.

"I think you're right. I might as well wait until it passes."

Laura picked up his glass and brought it to him. A moment later, they were back on the couch.

Still later, after the champagne was all gone and the rain had stopped, Alec and Laura looked at each other's disheveled appearance and laughed. Their impulsive moment of passion had passed as quickly as the squall that brought them together.

Back home, Alec checked his voice mail and listened to a message from Donna, the girl who had stolen Spencer's DVD.

"I just wanted to tell you how much I appreciate your advice about hospice. A really nice lady came by to see me that same afternoon. She was with us for almost two hours and afterward, we agreed Grandma would be better cared for in their facility in Fort Lauderdale. She knew exactly what to say to Grandma so she wouldn't be afraid." Her voice broke. "Anyway, I wanted to let you know that she passed away early this morning. Thank you, Mr. Santana. I'll never forget what you did for me, and for my grandma."

CHAPTER 27

As if on cue, a lone guitarist in the corner of the stage began to play a slow, somber piece that evoked images of a bullfight in slow motion. He played faster and louder as a young, dark-haired woman wearing a pink ruffled dress, made her entrance. With one hand curved above her head and the other below her waist she struck a dramatic pose that left little doubt she was the star of the show. Soon she was joined by the rest of cast—two men and two women—who took positions on either side of her. They danced *fandangos, farrucas* and *sevillanas* and when they were through, stomped off the stage as the music continued to play in the background.

"Bravo, Bravo!" shouted the dance director and a sprinkling of guests scattered throughout the small theater.

From the back, Alec made his way down the aisle and approached one of the female ushers. "I'm looking for Mrs. Goldstein. I was told she would be here today."

"She's backstage," the young usher said. "If you want, I can take you there."

"Thanks." He followed her to the end of the stage, up some stairs and to a private area behind the curtains. Mrs. Goldstein was talking with Sofia, the girl in the pink ruffled dress.

"Mrs. Goldstein, this gentleman would like to speak with you," said the usher. She waited a second, then turned and went back the same way she had come.

"I'm Alec Santana." He extended his hand.

"And this is Sofia." Mrs. Goldstein placed a protective arm around the girl's shoulder. "We've been expecting you. Why don't we go into one of the dressing rooms? We have a lot to discuss." She led the way to a room filled with costumes and large boxes stacked against a wall.

They sat and began to talk. "I don't know how much you were told about our problem," Mrs. Goldstein said, "but the fact is, you're our only hope. The police have basically given up on us."

"Why don't we start from the beginning?" Alec turned to Sofia. He pulled out a small notepad. "Tell me everything that happened."

Sofia took a deep breath. "Well, I got the first phone call about four and a half weeks ago. I didn't recognize the voice, but he sounded young, like he was close to my age. He said he'd been watching me and that he knew all about me, where I lived, what kind of car I drove and even my favorite foods."

"Have you actually seen him?"

"A couple of times I thought I saw someone following me on the way home after I left the studio, but I wasn't sure. The first time he drove a metallic green Grand Am with a pair of large dice hanging from the rearview mirror and the second time it was a white car, a Toyota, I think."

"Did you see who was driving?"

"No, but it was definitely a man wearing dark glasses. Unfortunately that's all I can remember."

Alec put his note pad aside. "Okay, let's talk about some possible suspects. Is there anyone you can think of who may want to harm you, or just want to scare you, for one reason or another? An old boyfriend, an admirer, anyone at all?"

Sofia shook her hand. "I've thought about it a lot, but to be honest, I can't think of a single person. I'm convinced that whoever it is, he's not someone I've had any dealings with, at least not in the recent past."

"You should know, Mr. Santana that this whole thing is taking its toll on her," Mrs. Goldstein said. "We're scheduled to take the show on a six city tour beginning next month and if we don't get to the bottom of this fairly soon…" She sighed. "Well, I don't know what we're going to do."

Sofia's lips quivered. "She's right. It's affecting my dancing and if it gets any worse, I think I'd rather quit. I'd hate to give up what I worked so hard to accomplish but I also want to do what's best for the company. I've already talked with the other dancers and they've been very supportive."

"Just so I'm clear, the caller has never threatened you in any way, is that correct?" Alec said.

"That's right." Sofia nodded. "He calls almost every day, usually on my cell phone, but sometimes at home. He enjoys dropping little tidbits about me, like the perfume I wear, the kind of music I listen to, things like that. He's getting to me and he knows it."

"Why haven't you just hung up on him?"

"I started doing that, but the detective who came to see me after Mrs. Goldstein called the police, told me not to. He thought if I let him talk, he might reveal something about himself, something that could give us a clue as to who he might be. So far he hasn't said very much, at least, nothing I would consider significant. The calls are very short and he usually begins by saying he saw me yesterday or a few hours ago. Then he rambles about stuff that doesn't make any sense. Other times he makes sexual remarks about my breasts or about some kinky fantasy that he had about me. When he's done he simply hangs up."

"The detective also said that unless the caller made some kind of real threat, there was nothing they could do," Mrs. Goldstein said. "As you can imagine, that wasn't what we wanted to hear."

Alec nodded. "I'm beginning to understand."

"Good." Mrs. Goldstein smiled. "Laura had great things to say about you and we're counting on you to get to the bottom of this. If there's anything we can do to help—"

"As a matter of fact there is. I'll need a complete list of all the cast members, with addresses and phone numbers. Sofia, I'd like to take a different approach, if you don't mind. From now on, every time he calls, just hang up. Don't say anything. Also, keep a log of the dates and times."

"You think he'll simply stop calling?" Mrs. Goldstein said.

"Not right away. What I want to do is force him to try something else, something riskier than what he's done so far." He handed Sofia a business card with his cell phone number. "Call me if anything happens or if you get nervous and just want to talk, okay?"

"Thanks," Sofia said. She hesitated. "Do you think you'll catch him, I mean, before the tour begins?"

He crossed his arms. "Until I know what I'm up against, it's hard to say." He half-smiled. "Remember, we're in this together, so keep your chin up. I have a feeling everything's going to be okay. I guess that's it." He got up. "I'll be in touch. Mrs. Goldstein, in the meantime, why don't you tell everyone why I'm here and that I want to speak to them. By the way, I thought you were great, Sofia."

Alec hung around to talk to the other dancers, including Sofia's best friend, Raquel. She recalled having seen someone lurking in the parking lot near the theater about a week before Sofia started getting the phone calls.

"Do you remember what he looked like?"

"He was a tall black guy, between twenty and twenty five years old. What got my attention was that he was wearing a trench coat, which nobody wears around here, not even in the winter. He gave me a long, hard look as I walked to my car. When I pulled away, I checked my rearview mirror and saw him get into a blue Mazda. For a second I thought he was going to follow me, but he turned in the opposite direction and I never saw him again."

"Did you tell this to the police?"

"Yes, and I also told Mrs. Goldstein. You think he might be the one, the guy who's harassing Sofia?"

"I don't know, but I'm going to find out. Do me a favor, if you remember anything else, no matter how insignificant, write it down, or better yet, give me a call."

CHAPTER 28

Two days later, Sofia called. Someone had taped a note to her windshield. He rushed over to see her.

Sitting on the couch in her living room, he read the short, hand printed note.

Why are you hanging up on me? Is it because you think you're too good for me? Well, I've got news for you. You're a has-been. Your dancing days are over. Why don't you do the world a favor and hang up your shoes?

"Why is he doing this to me?" Sofia said, her voice trembling. "I want it to be over, but it keeps getting worse." She shook her head. "I'll be honest with you, I don't know how much more I can take."

Using his thumb and forefinger Alec carefully placed the note in a large envelope. "Look, Sofia, I know how you feel, but you can't back down now. Don't you see? He's doing exactly what I thought he would. He's come out from under his rock and gave us the first real piece of evidence. I don't know what it means right now. It could be nothing; then again, it could be a significant clue about his personality, and more importantly, his motive."

"What if he tries something else? The note is one thing but—"

"We'll deal with it," he said firmly. "Just keep to your normal routine and try not to act frightened." He paused for a second. "It wouldn't be a bad idea if you checked your rearview mirror a little more often."

Her eyes opened wide. "You think he might try to follow me, like he did before?"

He shrugged. "I don't know. Just be extra careful whenever you leave the apartment, and keep your cell phone handy. By the way, I may be watching from a distance, so don't be surprised if you see me."

"I'm glad you told me. That makes me feel a lot better. So, what next?"

"Well, keep doing what you're doing. If he calls, hang up. We want to keep the ball on his court as much as possible. Before I forget, is there a possibility the guy you saw, the one who was following you, was black? The reason I ask is because Raquel said she saw a suspicious black guy hanging around the parking lot near the theater a few weeks ago."

Sofia thought about it for a moment. "The guy was white or maybe Latino, but definitely not black."

"By the way, who's your backup dancer?"

"Raquel."

After leaving Sofia's apartment, Alec couldn't get the last words of the note out of his mind. If what he was thinking were true...

He headed west toward Raquel's house in Hialeah where he parked at the end of the street and prepared to wait. He broke off after almost two hours to get some gas and a bottle of water.

He returned a half hour later and parked at the opposite end of the street. Within minutes, a metallic green Grand Am pulled into the driveway of Raquel's house. A young Latino in his mid-twenties got out and walked up to the door. His camera at the ready, Alec snapped one picture after another.

"Gotcha," he said under his breath as Raquel came out, kissed the young man hello, and then let him into the house.

Later, Alec called Mrs. Goldstein to let her know what he'd found. They agreed to meet at the Colony Theater tomorrow morning around eleven.

When he got home he listened to a cryptic voice mail message from Sergeant Carter. "About an interesting development in the Johnson murders," he emphasized.

Alec picked up the phone and dialed Carter's number. "I got your message. What's up?"

"Thought you'd want to know we found the Jackson brothers."

"Good job. Are they talking? Did you ask them about Victor?"

"Let me put it this way. They had nothing to say, not now, not ever. And they won't be needing a lawyer."

"You don't mean—"

"Yup. They were found in an east Georgia farmhouse with their hands tied behind their backs and bullet holes in the back of their heads. There were a couple of scales and some cocaine residue on the floor, so the locals are treating it like a drug deal gone bad. I'd say this pretty much shoots your wild conspiracy theory right out of the water."

"So what are you going to do? Just because somebody killed them doesn't mean they weren't working for Victor. Maybe you should—"

"Look, Alec. Take my advice. Forget about it and get yourself a different hobby. As far as I'm concerned the Johnson case is closed. They were all dopers, plain and simple, and they probably got what they deserved, except Mrs. Johnson. Poor lady just happened to be in the wrong place at the wrong time. Well, like I said, I thought you'd want to know."

Alec let out a quiet sigh. Carter's mind was all made up and there was no point trying to change it. He hung up and called Cecil to see how he was doing. His wife answered and he chatted with her for a moment until she passed the phone to Cecil.

"I'm glad you called," Cecil said. "I've been thinking about our last conversation at the hospital—about us working together. I wanted to talk about it some more when you have time. Maybe we can speed things up a little."

"It sounds like you're back to normal. What did the doctor say?"

"He says I'm fine. But he wants me to take it easy and hang around the house for the next few days. I'm driving my wife crazy, as you can imagine. She won't even let me help her do things. So when can you come over?"

Alec thought about it for a second. "I've got to meet a client in the morning. When I'm done, I can head over to your place."

"Great, I'll have a cold Corona waiting for you."

"By the way, I just got off the phone with Sergeant Carter, the deputy in charge of the Johnson Murders. You're not going to believe what happened. The main suspects, the Jackson brothers, were found dead in an east Georgia farmhouse. They think it was drug related. So now Carter is more convinced than ever that Johnson was just another drug dealer who got what he deserved. The case is officially closed."

"I don't know about you but I sure find it interesting that these good ole boys got killed soon after someone drops a dime on them. Pretty damn convenient, I'd say."

"Too convenient." Alec nodded. "This means Victor's going to get away with it and there's nothing I can do." He sighed. "Maybe Laura's right. I should stop thinking about it and try to concentrate on building up my business. Still, when I think of everything that's happened, I don't know if I can totally put it out of my mind. Just the other day I was going over the stuff from the evidence folder when they saved Victor from the burning fire. It made me sick knowing the person responsible for the death of Ben and the other ex-cops will get away with murder."

"I have an idea. When you come over, why don't you bring everything you have and let me take a look at it? I'm stuck here all day. It'll give me something to do besides watch the soaps and old sitcoms."

"Sure, I'll bring it over." The oven timer rang. "Gotta go. My TV dinner is done. See you tomorrow."

CHAPTER 29

"It's hard to believe." Mrs. Goldstein looked over the photographs. She held them up to the lights from the dresser mirror. "Are you sure about this?"

"I can't prove it, of course, but I'd stake my reputation on it," Alec said. "Let me explain. After I read the note that someone had left on Sofia's car, I knew it wasn't an ordinary stalker."

"What do you mean?" She put the photos aside.

"Well, whoever wrote it tipped his hand by mentioning Sofia's dancing. Up until now, there didn't appear to be a motive. It wasn't much of a clue, mind you, but it was enough to get me thinking about Raquel as a possible suspect, especially after learning she was Sofia's backup dancer." He picked up one of the photos and pointed to the car. "There aren't many metallic green Grand Ams with large dice hanging from the rearview mirror just like Sofia described. And the guy is about the right age, all of which tells me the odds are pretty damn good Raquel and her boyfriend are behind this."

"All right, so what do you propose we do?"

"Basically, we have two choices. Either I confront Raquel myself or we turn everything over to the police and let them handle it."

She stood next to a coat rack on which a pair of black leotards hung from a hook. "Now that we know it was an inside job, so to speak, we can't afford the bad publicity. So we definitely don't want to turn it over to the police. As for the second option, I'll have to think about it."

"It's up to you, but I wouldn't wait too long. There's no telling what they might try next."

"You're right," she said after a thoughtful pause. "We can't afford to wait. Raquel should be confronted as soon as possible. But I'd rather do it myself in my own way."

Alec raised an eyebrow. "You sure you want to do that?"

Mrs. Goldstein nodded. "Yes, I'm sure. I've known Raquel since she was a teenager and I've got a pretty good idea how I'm going to approach this. This means there's really nothing more for you to do, Mr. Santana. I think you did an excellent job, and I wouldn't hesitate to recommend you."

"Well, I guess that's it then," he said, unable to hide his disappointment. He would have enjoyed seeing Raquel's face the moment she saw the pictures. But it was Mrs. Goldstein's call and he had no choice but to accept it. "If you change your mind, you've got my number."

Kathy greeted Alec at the door and showed him to the den where Cecil sat watching a game show. He sat in his favorite easy chair with his feet stretched over a footstool.

"Good to see you," Cecil said, without getting up. He grabbed the remote and pressed the Off key. "Make yourself comfortable. Honey, why don't you bring us a couple of beers?"

"See what I have to put with?" She smiled. "Ever since he got home from the hospital, it's been honey can you get me this, honey can you get me that. He's milking the doctor's orders not to overexert himself just a little too much." She laughed. "But I'm not complaining. Two cold beers coming up." She turned to leave the room.

"Well, you look good." Alec took a seat across from him. He placed a folder containing the papers Irene had given him on the coffee table. "When are you going back to work?"

"Today has been my best day yet. If I feel this good tomorrow, I might go to the lab for at least part of the day."

"I'm glad you're feeling better. So what's this about you wanting to move up our plans? What's the rush, anyway? What I mean is, you're the one that stands to lose if the idea goes bust for one reason or another. If I were you I'd think about it some more. Have you talked it over with Kathy? I wouldn't want her to think I'm trying to push you into this."

Cecil sighed. "She knows all about it. Unfortunately she's dead set against it. But I've made up my mind and, well, we've stopped fighting about it. She'll come around, eventually. Of course I'll have to give my boss at least a couple of weeks notice."

"I don't know." Alec shook his head. "Maybe you should listen to her."

Kathy appeared with the two beers, set them down on the coffee table and returned to the kitchen.

Alec picked up a bottle and waited for Cecil to do the same. "*Salud.*" He lifted the bottle and took a quick gulp.

"You haven't changed your mind, have you?" Cecil said.

"Of course not, I think we'd make a damn good team. In fact I purposely leased a larger office with you in mind. It's just off West Dixie Highway."

"For a moment I thought you were going to try to talk me out of it."

"It wouldn't do any good." Alec chuckled. "You've obviously given it a lot of thought. Just let me know when you're ready to come over." His cell phone rang. "Hold on a moment."

"Bonnie, I'm surprised to hear from you." He listened as she gave him an update on Sharon's baby. "Okay, so what happens next?" He nodded, and then smiled. "Thanks, I owe you big time."

"That was Bonnie, a Broward County Sheriff's deputy. She and I used to…well, I'll tell you all about it sometime. Anyway, she had some good news about an orphaned baby who's about to be put up for adoption." He filled him in on the details of Irene Bailey's daughter, and then stood to leave. "I have to run over and see Irene. She has a good chance to adopt her daughter's baby, but she's got to move fast."

Alec rang the bell and knocked on the door. No response. Disappointed, he left a note for Irene to call him the moment she got in.

He didn't hear from her until late in the afternoon. She'd just gotten back from Orlando where her she'd gone to visit her sister.

"I'm sorry I missed you," Alec said. "I really wanted to tell you in person. Are you sitting down?"

"What is it?"

"Sharon's family has decided to give up the baby for adoption. It's not going to be easy, but if you move quickly and make a claim based on being a blood relative, they should at least give you preference."

Irene started to cry. "It's like God is giving me a second chance. Thank you, Mr. Santana. You made this possible and I'll never forget you."

Alec gave her Bonnie's phone number. "She's a good friend of mine. She'll tell you everything you need to do. By the way, the baby's name is Heather. Good luck, and let me know how everything turns out."

The phone rang a second later; he picked it up in mid ring.

"You're not supposed to know this," Laura said, "but Mrs. Goldstein plans to give you a generous bonus on top of your fee. Nice going. If you keep this up, you're going to be a rich man."

Alec laughed. "Me rich? I wouldn't know how to handle it."

"Don't knock it. It beats the alternative, otherwise known as having to live on a budget. Anyway, I just wanted to congratulate you on a job well done and…to invite you over for a mini-celebration."

"Right now?"

"Sure, it's still early. I even stocked my refrigerator with a few bottles of beer, just for you."

"Can I take a rain check? I promised Julie I'd take her out for dinner. She went to the cemetery this afternoon and she's feeling kind of down."

"Okay, but don't wait too long, otherwise I might think you're trying to avoid me."

He chuckled. "I'll call you soon, I promise. On second thought, I might surprise you and show up unexpectedly."

CHAPTER 30

Alec left for his office a little before 9:00 a.m., stopped to pick up coffee and a doughnut and pulled into the parking lot twenty minutes later.

He found Cecil waiting in the hallway. "You must really be anxious to come on board. Were we supposed to meet here or something?"

"I tried to reach you at home, but you had already left." He held the folder with the papers that Alec had left for him to examine. "I was feeling pretty good, so I decided to drive over and tell you in person."

Alec looked at him. "Tell me what?" He fumbled for his keys and unlocked the door.

"You were right." Cecil followed Alec into the office. "After you left, I went over the stuff in the folder. There was nothing there, at least nothing obvious or significant."

"You came here just to tell me I was right? You feeling okay?" He walked around the desk and sat down.

Cecil continued, "I had everything out on my work table in the bedroom. I left it there, thinking I might go over it one more time. But I didn't get a chance until early this morning. I was holding a cup of coffee and accidentally spilled a few drops on the map of Argentina I had been looking at. When I blotted them with a towel, I looked down and suddenly froze. There it was staring me in the face, half an inch below one of the drops. ROSARIO."

"What are you talking about?"

Cecil pulled out the map and spread it across Alec's desk. He put his finger on Rosario, a city northwest of Buenos Aires.

Alec leaned over to get a better look. "Well, I'll be damned."

Cecil smiled. "Are you ready for the good part? I researched Victor's family and guess what? They come from the city of Rosario. That's what Ben Brody was referring to. It was never a woman's name, that's why nobody ever heard of her."

Alec repeated Ben's message. "'Rosario holds all the answers.' It's possible, I suppose. If only we knew what Ben was trying to tell us." He leaned back in his chair and thought about it for a moment. "You know what this means, don't you? I'm back on the case."

"So where do we start?" Cecil took a seat across from Alec's desk.

"We? First things first. You have to take care of yourself and then get back to work and give them notice like you said you would."

"You're right," Cecil said, disappointed. "But I'll be available if you need me."

Alec reached into the bag with the coffee and doughnut. "I've never been to Argentina. It'll probably cost a fortune in airfare. But if I don't go down there to see what Ben was trying to tell me, I know I'll regret it later." He removed the lid from the coffee container and took a quick sip.

"Well, it's not going to be easy. It might even be dangerous. The moment you start asking questions about Victor, word will spread quickly and you may find yourself in a heap of trouble." He shook his head. "I don't know...maybe you should wait a couple of weeks. By then I should know what I'm doing, and if everything goes well, we can go down there together."

"I appreciate the offer, but I want to get this over with, the sooner the better. We have a P.I. business to get off the ground, remember?"

Cecil smiled. "You bet." He looked around the large, rectangular room that had two of everything: two desks, two chairs, two filing cabinets and two aerial photographs of Miami Beach. "Don't take this the wrong way, Alec, but I think the place could use a little sprucing up. You mind if I have

Kathy come over and change things around, maybe add some curtains and a few plants? She's got a good eye for knowing what goes with what, and it wouldn't even cost much. What do you think?"

Alec shrugged. "I guess it does look a little spartan. Sure, why not?" He smiled. "Just as long as she doesn't get carried away. We don't want it to look like a law office. You know what I mean? The last thing we want is to be confused with a couple of down-and-out lawyers."

Later, Alec made flight and hotel reservations, and then went through all the items in the folder, especially the latest information that Cecil had found. He picked up an old photograph of Victor and his parents and stared at it for a long moment.

The phone rang. He waited a second before answering it.

"They found Jeff's body." Laura sounded as though she'd been crying.

"When? Where?"

"It washed up near Palm Beach yesterday morning. I don't know why but the news really got to me. Even though we were probably going to split up, I did love the guy, in a peculiar sort of way. I know it doesn't make sense." She sighed. "I hate to admit it but I was hoping they'd never find him. I'd like to have a memorial service for him as soon as possible, maybe even tomorrow, rather than wait for the Medical Examiner to release the body."

"Sounds like you could use some company. If you want I can be there in half an hour."

"I appreciate it, but I have a lot of feelings to sort out. It's best if I do it alone. Why don't you call me in the morning and maybe we can meet for coffee."

"I'm afraid I can't make it, at least not tomorrow. I've got a plane to catch…to Argentina." He filled her in on what Cecil had uncovered. "I know it may turn out to be a wild goose chase, but if I don't do it now, I might not do it at all."

"This is crazy, Alec. You said you wanted to put it behind you so you could concentrate on your business. Personally I think you're making a mistake. Besides, nobody cares about it, certainly not the police. You proved that Ben was no thief. Isn't that enough?"

"I guess not," he said after a long pause. "There are just too many unanswered questions, and maybe I'll be able to find some answers. It may sound corny, but I think Ben would want me to do this."

"Well, you've obviously made up your mind. All I can say is good luck. And be careful. Call me when you get back."

CHAPTER 31

From the airport, Alec made a last minute call to Cecil. No answer. He tried again a minute later and Cecil answered on the second ring.

"I hope I didn't wake you," Alec said.

"It's six-fifteen in the morning, for God's sake. Of course you woke us. I didn't expect to hear from you until you arrived in Argentina."

"I was going to call last night, but it was late and I still had a lot of things to do." He paused. "Listen, are you ready for this? A couple of days ago they found Conway's body near Palm Beach. Laura called me yesterday afternoon and told me all about it."

"So much for the theory that he took the money and ran off to some faraway place. How is Laura taking it?"

"It was a shock, of course, but I think she'll be okay. Don't forget, she had already decided to divorce him." He hesitated. "She's planning on having a memorial service for him. If it's not too much trouble, can you find out where it will be and maybe drop by to pay our respects? It would mean a lot to Laura and to me as well."

"Sure, no problem. Where will you be staying, in case I need to reach you?"

"The Castelar Hotel in Buenos Aires. I'll rent a car and drive out to Rosario first thing tomorrow morning."

"Well, I'm sure I don't have to tell you to be careful. Once Victor knows you're in town there's no telling what he might try to do. I sure wish you were packing."

"Yeah, me too." A loudspeaker blared out a boarding call. "That's my flight. I'll call you when I get to Rosario. Wish me luck." He hung up and joined a line of passengers, moving quickly toward an open doorway.

In Buenos Aires, Alec rented a car and drove to his hotel near the center of town. He spent the rest of the afternoon going over the articles in the folder and inquiring about Rosario.

"We're here and there's Rosario," said the concierge, his finger sliding across a large map. He marked it with a black felt pen to show the best route to take. "You should leave as early as possible if you plan to return the same day. I used to live there and go back to visit my family at least once a month."

"Then you must know the streets pretty well." Alec hesitated, and then pulled out a three by five card with the name Victor Cardini and an old address written on it. "You know where this is?" He held the card up to him.

The man nodded. "Sure, it's on a narrow street, near a church and a small park." He moved his finger to a smaller map of Rosario. Using the same pen, he drew a circle around the general area. "Just look for the church and you'll know you're close to the address."

"Thanks, I appreciate it." Brief pause. "By the way, could you recommend a good restaurant?"

"La Fogata, just down the street. They have the best *Parrillada* in town. If you like pasta, be sure and ask for the *fettucine carbonara*. Tell them I sent you and they'll give you a complimentary drink."

Alec thanked him again and left.

The concierge waited until Alec was well beyond earshot, picked up the phone and dialed a number.

"Hello?" answered a man with a husky voice.

"It's Emilio. I thought you'd want to know a man was just here asking for directions to Rosario. He had Victor Cardini's name and an old address."

"Who is he?"

"He checked in a few hours ago under the name Alec Santana, from Miami, Florida. He'll probably drive to Rosario first thing in the morning."

"Do me a favor. Keep an eye on him and let me know if he meets with anyone."

"Sure thing. I'll call you the moment I see anything unusual."

The next day Alec got up early and made the long drive to Rosario, a bustling city about 190 miles northwest of Buenos Aires, on the western shore of the Parana River. Victor's last known address turned out to be a high-rise building facing a small park. Pulling into the lot Alec didn't notice a gray Volvo that had been following him from a distance. It stayed back and parked near a side street, several yards from the entrance.

Alec entered the building, paused to check the directory, and then took the elevator to the third floor. The address was at least fifteen years old; he'd be lucky if anyone remembered the family. He knocked on the door to Apartment 3B.

Seconds later, an old woman wearing a lavender robe and matching slippers opened the door.

"Sorry to bother you," Alec said, "but I'm looking for a family that used to live in this apartment many years ago. Their name was Cardini and they had a little boy named Victor. Can you tell me if—"

The old woman shook her head. "I'm sorry, but I moved here a year ago, shortly after my husband died. You may want to try another apartment." She started to close the door. "The man who lives in 3J. I don't know his name, but I was told he's lived there almost twenty years."

"*Gracias.*" Alec turned around and walked down the hallway. He heard a familiar tango coming from apartment 3J as he rang the bell. Seconds later, the music stopped and the door opened slowly.

"Yes, can I help you?" said a tall, slender man who looked to be about seventy. He had mostly silver hair combed to the back and wore a gray, thin moustache that complemented his long, wedge-like face.

"I'm sorry to bother you, but I was told you might be able to help me. I'm looking for a family that lived in apartment 3B a long time ago. Their name was Cardini. Do you remember them by any chance?"

The man thought about it for a moment. "Yes, I do remember them. They lived here for about two or three years. The last I heard they had moved to the United States."

"I know it's been a long time, but do you know if they had any relatives? They may have lived in this building or somewhere nearby."

A look of suspicion formed on the man's face. "Why do you want to know?"

Alec hesitated. He had to come up with something halfway believable. "You see, I was hired by the family of a distant cousin from New York who died several weeks ago. In his will he named several members of the Cardini family and that's why I'm trying to locate them."

The old man shrugged. "They kept to themselves and I really couldn't say whether they had other relatives. Have you tried the church across the street? There's a priest. Father Federico has been there at least twenty years. He knows almost everyone in the neighborhood, especially the ones who keep the faith. If they attended Mass, I'm sure he'd remember them."

"*Muchas Gracias.* You've been very helpful." He left the building and walked across the street to a small church that looked as though it was undergoing renovation. He entered quietly so as not to disturb the dozen or so people, mostly old women, who sat in pews or knelt before the altar.

A cleaning woman emerged from a side door. He stepped toward her. "I'm looking for Father Federico. Can you tell me where I might find him?"

"He's in the courtyard tending his roses. It's in the back, next to the rectory."

"*Gracias.*" Alec walked out and went around to the back.

"I can see you have a green thumb, Father." Alec looked over a small garden of mostly red roses planted next to a tall, crumbling statue of St. Francis of Assisi. "They're absolutely beautiful."

"They are indeed." He sprinkled them with water from a can, ever so gently, as though he were blessing them. "They're like my children and I take good care of them." He stopped what he was doing. "I don't think I've seen you before. Are you new to the parish?"

"No, I'm just a visitor. My name is Alec Santana from Miami and I'm looking for relatives of a family, the Cardinis that used to live in this neighborhood." He repeated the story he'd told the man in apartment 3J. "I know it's been many years, but do you remember them at all?"

Father Federico sighed slowly. "I remember them well. It was a terrible shock when I heard that José and Paloma were killed in a fire in the United States. After it happened, I thought about Victor, their son, and worried that he was alone with no one to care for him. Then about a week or two later, I heard that his uncle had gone to Miami to bring him back to Argentina. I never met the uncle and I don't know his name or anything else about him." He gave a small shrug. "I know I haven't been much help, but that's all I can remember."

"This uncle that brought Victor back to Argentina…do you know if he lived in Rosario?"

"I'm not sure, but I think he did. The reason I say this is because a parishioner, a woman who died a few years ago, happened to mention that she had run into Victor and his uncle at a local clinic. Apparently the boy suffered from severe asthma. As I recall, this was about a year and a half after they came back from Miami."

"Do you think Victor and his uncle might still be around?"

"I doubt it. The last I heard was that the uncle had taken the boy to Buenos Aires where he could get better treatment. That was years ago and I'm sorry to say I don't know what became of them."

"Well, I guess that's it then," Alec said, disappointed. "I had hoped to find at least one member of the Cardini family, but I can see it's not going to be that easy. Thank you for your time, Father." He shook the priest's hand and then turned and left the courtyard.

The man in the gray Volvo watched Alec get into his car and pull out of the parking lot. When he drove by, he cranked his engine and followed from a distance. He stayed with him all the way back to Buenos Aires.

In his room, Alec spotted a flashing red light on the side of the phone. He had a voice mail message.

"You were supposed to call me when you got to Rosario." Cecil sounded like a worried parent. "I need to know what's going on. Call me the moment you get this message."

Alec smiled as he grabbed a beer from the mini bar and sat down on the bed. A minute later he picked up the phone and dialed Cecil's number.

"I just got back from Rosario," Alec said, the moment he heard Cecil's voice.

"So how did it go?"

Alec took a long swig of his beer. "It may have been a good place to start, but Rosario sure didn't hold any answers, at least not that I could find. An old priest who knew Victor's family said that Victor and an uncle had moved to Buenos Aires years ago. So if he's here, it's going to be a lot harder that I had anticipated."

"How long are you going to give it?"

"I don't know. The truth is I have no real plan. I thought about going to the police, but what am I going to tell them? That they have a dangerous psychopath loose in the city and that I'm here to find him?" He sighed. "Maybe it was a mistake to even come here."

"Well, whatever you do, keep me posted. I'm supposed to be your partner, remember? By the way, I went to Conway's memorial service. I met his widow and she was just as I imagined—tall, beautiful and elegant." He chuckled. "I don't know what she sees in you, but if I were you I'd snatch her up in a minute."

"The truth is, I'm basically a beer and steak man and she's more the caviar and champagne type. I just don't think it would work. Besides, her money would eventually come between us, which is what probably happened with her and Conway." He paused.

"Hold on, I hear something." The corner of an envelope appeared under the door. He dashed out into the hallway. Nobody there. He went back inside, picked up the envelope and pulled out a handwritten note. Holding it in his hand, Alec read the message to Cecil.

> *If you want to know about Victor and where you can find him, meet me in front of the Boca Juniors Stadium tomorrow morning at ten. I'll be in a white VW. Come alone and bring plenty of cash."*

"I know you want to get to the bottom of this, but it could be trap," Cecil said. "My advice is to let this one pass."

"And then what? Wait for him to contact me again?" He shook his head. "I just want to get this over with. One way or another, I want to know the truth about Victor, about everything."

"Okay. Do what you have to do. Just do me a favor. Tell someone—anyone—where you're going to be. And for God's sake, don't forget to—"

"I know," Alec said, mildly annoyed. "I'll call when it's over."

CHAPTER 32

Alec arrived early and parked in plain view near the entrance to the stadium. He saw maintenance workers going in and out and it made him feel safe, but not for long. At almost ten o'clock, a white VW pulled up alongside him. The driver, a stocky, middle-aged man wearing jeans and a tan windbreaker, got out and waited for Alec to do the same. The man carried a small leather bag.

Alec glanced around and took note of a gray Volvo parked directly across the street.

"Did you bring the money?" said the man.

"Not so fast," Alec answered. "You said you knew about Victor and where I could find him."

"That's right. I can take you to him. Let's see the cash."

Alec looked at him for a second. "Who are you anyway? How did you know I was looking for Victor?"

"That's not important. Let's just say I have sources who keep me well informed. If we're through with the questions, why don't we get in my car and I'll show you where Victor hangs out."

"Just tell me where it is and if I think you're telling the truth I'll—"

The man reached into his bag, pulled out a Beretta and pointed it at Alec. "Like I said, why don't we get in my car? Go ahead, get in, but do it slowly, no sudden movements."

"Hey, take it easy, all right." Alec stared at the pistol. "If it's the money you want, you can have it. You can have it all. I've got almost five hundred dollars on me and it's yours." He reached for his wallet.

"Stop right there. Just get in the car."

"Don't you want the money?"

"I changed my mind. Now get in the car and do it quickly."

Alec hesitated. "Whatever you say." He took a couple of steps toward the VW and paused when he saw the gray Volvo barreling toward them.

Startled, the man in the windbreaker turned and momentarily took his eyes off Alec.

Alec lunged directly at him and tried to wrestle the gun from his hand. In the scuffle, the gun went off and grazed the man in his side. Frightened, the man jumped in his car and took off just as the Volvo appeared.

The driver got out. "Are you all right?" His eyes darted between Alec and the VW that sped away.

"I'm okay," Alec said, trying to catch his breath. "I don't know where you came from, but you saved my life. Thanks."

"I was across the street and saw the whole thing. Was he trying to rob you?"

"Yeah, I guess so."

The man looked at him carefully. "You're not from around here, are you? I can tell by your accent."

"No, I'm not. Look, I don't mean to be rude but I've got to get going." He stepped toward his car.

"You're wasting your time. You're not going to find him."

Alec stopped in his tracks. "What are you talking about?"

"Victor Cardini. Isn't that why you came here?"

"You were following me, weren't you? Who are you, anyway? Are you working for Victor?"

The man took a moment to answer. "Why don't we take a drive? There's something you should see."

"You're the second guy today who's asked me to go for a drive." He backed off. "No offense, but I think I'll pass."

"Look, if I wanted to harm you I could have done it on the way to Rosario, or I could have just let the man shoot you. If you'll feel safer, you can follow me. It's up to you." The man gave him a couple of seconds, and then turned to get in his car.

Alec didn't say anything as he got in his own car and waited for the man to pull out. Against his better judgment, he cranked the engine and followed him from a safe distance.

Forty minutes later, the Volvo reached its destination in a rural area near the edge of the city. Alec was right behind him and they got out of their cars simultaneously.

"Is this some kind of joke?" Alec said, his eyes focused on a large marble statue of the risen Christ standing near the entrance to a Catholic Cemetery.

"Please follow me," the man said without explaining further. He led the way into the cemetery, which he seemed to know well, and walked around familiar monuments and markers. When he reached the one he had come to see, he paused and made a quick, almost involuntary sign of the cross.

Alec came around him and suddenly froze when he saw the name on the headstone:

VICTOR CESARE CARDINI
Junio 1983 - Septiembre 1997

"I-I don't know what to say," Alec stammered. "I came here hoping to meet him, to talk to him." He took a step backwards. "Wait a second, if Victor is dead, then you must be—"

The man nodded. "Yes, I'm Victor's uncle. My name is Hugo Montenegro. I think we should talk. There's a coffee shop across the street."

They sat next to a wall covered with photographs of celebrities from the past. Oddly missing was a picture of Eva Peron or her husband Juan. "Why were you following me?" Alec said, the moment the waiter delivered their coffees.

The man smiled. "Emilio, the concierge at your hotel is an old friend of mine and he called me the day you arrived. To be honest, I couldn't imagine what it was you were hoping to find, especially after all these years." He placed a heaping teaspoon of sugar into his coffee. "Then it occurred to me that maybe it had something to do with the money."

"The money?" Alec tried to play dumb.

"There was a rumor back then that Victor's father, who was married to my sister, was in possession of a large amount of money that was never recovered."

Alec took a sip of his coffee. "You think the rumor was true?"

The man shrugged. "So, if you didn't come for the money, what are you doing here?"

Alec glanced around the room. "Look, I wasn't going to say anything, but you did save my life, after all. You deserve to know what this is all about." He took a sip of his coffee, and then related everything that had happened from the day he found the crumpled pieces of paper, to his meeting with Johnson and finally to his arrival in Buenos Aires. After a long pause, he said, "It's pretty clear that somebody didn't want me to know the truth about Victor. All along, I was led to believe he was behind everything."

"Who would do such a thing?" the man said, his voice rising. "To use my nephew's name in such a way…it was a terrible, evil thing to do. It makes me sick just thinking about it."

Alec nodded. "You're right, and all I can say is that one way or another I intend to get to the bottom of this. I have a theory about who's behind it, but I won't know for sure until I get back to Miami and start asking questions."

"Well, if there's anything I can do to help—anything at all…" He pulled a business card from his shirt pocket and handed it to Alec. "It's a small book store that I own. You can reach me there anytime."

Alec glanced at the card briefly, and then looked at his watch. "If I hurry I might make the next flight to Miami."

CHAPTER 33

The waitress delivered the breakfast special for Cecil: two eggs, two strips of bacon, hash brown potatoes and Cuban toast. Alec had the same, minus the potatoes.

"Just wave to me if you want some more coffee." She looked Nicaraguan or maybe Honduran, with a soft honey complexion and a full-lipped mouth that reminded him of a young Sophia Loren.

"Thanks." Alec smiled. He kept his eyes on her as she sauntered off toward the kitchen.

"Quit looking at her ass and finish telling me about Victor."

"Sorry." Alec turned to Cecil. "Like I was saying, Victor's uncle didn't know much, though he did guess that it had to do with the money. He had heard about rumors that Victor's father was in possession of a large amount of money."

"So if Victor is dead and his uncle knew nothing about the scheme pretending that he was alive, where does that leave us?"

Alec took a sip of his coffee. "I wish I knew, but it's safe to say that whoever's behind this is probably here in Miami. And he had to know that sooner or later, I'd stumble upon the truth. That's why he set me up at the stadium."

"He?" Cecil said, digging into his breakfast. "Who are you talking about?"

Alec hesitated. "I'm talking about…" He shook his head. "It could be almost anyone. Anyone with a motive."

"You mean the money, don't you?"

"It's the best motive in the world. That's why I feel that unlike the others, Conway's death was no suicide. From the very beginning, the one thing that never set right with me was that he took the secret about the money's location to his grave. My guess is that he was either forced to reveal where the money was hidden or he had already dug into it and didn't want to share it."

Cecil put down his fork. "I'm getting a bad feeling about this. Maybe it's time to bring in some extra help, like the Florida Department of Law Enforcement or maybe even the Feds."

"What would we tell them?" Alec stared at Cecil for a long moment. "They'd never believe us. Besides, the first person they'd talk to is Detective Palafox, and we know what he's going to say. Look, as much as I want to find out who's behind this, I think we should put a lid on it, at least for a while. Sooner or later they'll make another move. When they do, we'll be ready for them."

"I don't know," Cecil said, his eyes blinking more rapidly than usual. "I still think we should—"

"Relax, will you? If you're going to be my partner, the first thing you have to learn is not to worry so much. Now let's finish our breakfast so we can get the hell out of here. I've got some calls to make and you've got to start getting ready to come on board. By the way, do you own a gun?"

Cecil swallowed hard. "A gun? Why…why would I need a gun?"

"With everything that's been happening lately, well, you never know when I might need backup." He caught a scared look from Cecil. "It's just a precaution. If you don't have one don't worry about it."

After breakfast, Alec drove to his office and spent the rest of the morning going over his mail and returning phone calls. On hold he heard someone trying to open the door, which was locked. He put the phone down, grabbed his gun from the drawer and stepped forward.

"Who's there?"

"It's me, Laura."

Alec breathed a sigh of relief and let her in. He put the gun back in the drawer and waited for her to take a seat.

"Do you greet all your visitors with a gun?" Laura said, her tone serious.

"I'm sorry, but ever since I got back from Argentina, I've been a little on edge. How did you know I was back?"

"I didn't. I was on my way to meet the owner of new gallery and happened to spot your car in the parking lot. You were supposed to call me, remember?" She softened her tone. "So, did you have any luck?"

Alec crossed his hands behind his head and leaned back in his chair. "I went there not really sure what to expect. I mean, I had very little to go on. Ben's cryptic message about Rosario, the fact Victor's family happened to be from the same town and—"

"Did you find the mysterious Victor?"

"I found him, all right, but he wasn't the one."

"What do you mean?"

Alec relaxed his hands. "The kid died years ago." He leaned forward. He told her about everything that happened, including his near fatal encounter with an armed stranger. "If it hadn't been for Victor's uncle showing up the way he did..." He shook his head. "Well, I'm just glad that he happened to be nearby."

"You're not going back there, I hope?"

"I have no reason to. The players are here in Miami, where they've been from the very beginning. I have a few theories though." He hesitated. "About the possibility that Jeff didn't commit suicide."

She looked at him for a moment. "What are you trying to say, that he was murdered? But why?"

"I can think of only one reason. The money. As to the who, well, it's anybody's guess. Only a few people knew about the money and they're all dead, which means that someone must've broken the pact and told at least one other person. I'm just guessing, mind you, but it's possible that whoever that person was had a hand in forcing Jeff to produce the money. I also have to assume it was no coincidence that everything started happening just a few months before the fifteen years were up."

"I don't know what to say. Maybe you're right, but it doesn't change the fact that it's water under the bridge. I mean, does it really matter? You cleared your friend's name and you found out that poor Victor had nothing to do with this." She shook her head. "You're not a cop, Alec. I think you should leave it alone and get back to being what you are—a private eye. Just look at you, the way you answered the door. Do you really want to live this way?"

"You sound like Cecil." Alec held back a smile. "He thinks I should turn it over to the State or the Feds, which I have no intention of doing." He picked up a pencil and twirled it with his fingers. "To be honest, I don't know what I'm going to do, mostly because I have very little to go on. Anyway, Cecil and I have a P.I. business to run so I may not have time to do anything else."

"Good." Laura's lips formed a smile. "And to make sure you stay busy I'm going to call a few friends. You know, the ones with the deep pockets? I guarantee you'll be so busy, you might even have to hire some extra help." She laughed. "Well, I've got to run. I'm late for my appointment."

"I'll walk you to your car." He grabbed his gun, slipped it into the hollow of his back and put on his coat. "It's my security blanket, all right?"

She smiled, but didn't say anything as she followed him out the door.

Back in his office, the phone rang. He picked it up on the third ring. He recognized Kathy's voice. "Everything all right?"

"I'm okay, but I'm worried about Cecil."

"He didn't have a relapse, did he?"

"No, he's fine." She hesitated. "The reason I'm calling is because…I don't know how to say this, but he is having second thoughts about quitting his job. Knowing him he's not going to mention it to you, so I guess I'm doing it for him."

"I don't understand. Did something happen to make him change his mind?"

"Well, sort of. I know it sounds silly, but this case you're working is getting to him. I mean really getting to him. And when you asked if he owned a gun, well, that finally did it. The truth is, he's not cut out to be a private eye. He's happiest in the lab where he belongs, but he doesn't want to disappoint you."

Alec nodded. "I think I know where you're coming from. You want me to talk to him? Is that it?"

"If it's not too much trouble. Maybe you could—"

"Say no more. I'll come up with something. One way or another I'll make him see that he's better off staying where he is."

"I knew I could count on you, Alec," she said, relief in her voice. "One more thing. I'd rather he not know I called."

"I understand. I'll call him in a few minutes. He'll never know that we had this conversation."

"You've been talking to Kathy, haven't you?" Cecil said, the moment Alec mentioned the lab and the good job he'd be leaving.

"No, of course not. I just want to make sure you're ready to do this. What I mean is that if you have any doubts, any doubts whatsoever, then don't do it."

"Sounds to me like you're the one with the doubts. About me. Look, if you've changed your mind about taking me on as your partner, then just say so. We've been friends too long to let anything come between us."

"You got it all wrong, Cecil. Of course I want you as a partner. The thing is, I've been thinking that maybe we should hold off doing anything until we're sure the business is in the black. So far, I've barely made enough money to cover my expenses. It wouldn't be fair of me to expect you to leave a nice comfortable job at the lab."

"Well, when you put it that way…"

"I've got an idea. Why don't you be an independent consultant? This way you could keep your job and work with me on a case by case basis. It would be like having your cake and eating it too. What do you say?"

There was a brief silence. "A consultant…hmm. I like the sound of that. Okay, you talked me into it."

"Good. Now let me get back to work. We'll talk more tomorrow, maybe over a cup of coffee."

CHAPTER 34

"**W**ho is this?" Alec said into the phone.

Dead silence.

"Look, if you don't tell me who you are—"

"I'm Patty Leblanc," said the caller, a woman with a shaky tone to her voice. "Ray Leblanc is my husband. Are you still working the case?" She waited a couple of seconds. "Well, are you?"

"Why are you calling and how did you get my name?"

"I want to know if you're working the case," she persisted. "Because if you are, I've got some information for you. I hate doing this, but my husband has left me no choice."

"I'm listening."

"Maybe we should talk in person. There's a bar in Dania called O'Malley's, just off South Federal Highway. I can be there in half an hour."

"How will I recognize you?"

"I know who you are. Just be there." She hung up before he could ask any more questions.

When Alec got to the bar, she was already there and she waved to him from her table in the corner of the room. He acknowledged her with a nod and made his way to where she was seated.

"I wasn't sure you'd make it," she said, her hand wrapped around a near empty glass. About fifty, with a plain, plumpish face, she wore small-framed glasses that made her face look even larger.

Alec took a seat across from her and signaled to a waitress who came right over. "I'll have a Guinness and another drink for the lady."

"Thanks. I think I'm going to need it." She downed the last of her drink and took a deep breath. "I want you to know I'm taking a big risk just being here. If my husband should ever find out…"

"I understand." Alec nodded. "You have my word that whatever you tell me will stay between us."

"Good. Now let me tell you what I know and why I think your life may be in danger. Are you aware that my husband has been keeping tabs on you? He even has a picture of you he took when you were coming out of Laura Conway's house."

"How do you know all of this?"

"I've overhead his conversations, usually when he's on the phone but sometimes when his friend Jim Palafox came to the house to visit him. I don't know what they're up to but they're worried about you, like you're a threat or something."

Alec stared at her for a moment. "I appreciate you telling me this, but what's your motive?"

She waited for the waitress to deliver their drinks. "He's leaving me for another woman. They say the wife is the last to know and they're right. After almost twenty years of what I thought was a pretty good marriage…" Her lips quivered. "Well, I'm sure you can fill in the rest."

"I'm sorry," Alec said after a brief pause. He reached for his beer. "Are you sure you want to continue?"

She nodded. "I'm a scorned woman and you know what they say. *Hell hath no fury…*" She picked up her glass and took a large gulp. "Are you ready for the good stuff?"

"I'm all ears." He leaned forward.

"About a month and a half ago, I found a business card in one of my husband's pants pockets when I was getting ready to wash them. I noticed a couple of phone numbers on the back. Well, the next day my husband starts rummaging through the clothes hamper. I asked what he was looking for, but he just ignored me. He had this really worried look his face, so I asked him again. When I told him I had washed them and hung them up, he looked at me as if he hadn't heard. Then he turned and left in a huff. If he'd asked me for the card, I would have just given it to him. But he didn't, so I naturally assumed he was hiding something from me."

She took another sip of her drink and continued. "To make a long story short, I called the numbers. I was curious to see if they were hers, the woman he's been seeing behind my back. But they weren't. They turned out to be the numbers for a couple of former cops my husband had worked with. In a way I was disappointed but I also felt a little foolish so I tore the card in half and threw it in the trashcan."

"Who were the ex-cops?"

"I was getting to that. They were Ben Brody and Stuart Mendoza. What happened next is what really got my attention. About five or six weeks later, I heard on the radio that Ben Brody had committed suicide and I thought, how sad, even though I barely remembered him. Then a week later, I read in the paper that Stuart Mendoza had also committed suicide. Coincidence?" She shrugged. "I don't pretend to know what's going on here, but in the days that followed, I overheard my husband mention their names during different phone calls. He sounded agitated, not grief-stricken, if you know what I mean."

Alec took a long sip of his beer. "Let me ask you something. Did your husband take a trip out of town about two weeks ago?"

Mrs. Leblanc thought about it for a moment. "As a matter of fact he did. He went up to St. Augustine to check out a boat someone was selling. At least that's what he told me."

"Do you know if he went alone?"

"I don't know. Palafox might have gone with him, I suppose."

"Does your husband own a shotgun?"

"He used to, but that was years ago. He said he sold it to some guy in Key West."

"What about a truck?"

"You mean, does he own one? No, but he has a cousin who has a used car lot on North West Twenty-Seventh Avenue. Majestic Motors it's called; it's about a mile north of the community college. In the past, my husband borrowed cars from there, sometimes for weeks. I don't remember a truck, though. If he drove one, he never parked it in our driveway." She took a large gulp of her drink. "You sure ask a lot of questions. My husband is in a lot of trouble, isn't he?"

Alec hesitated. "I don't know, maybe. Can you think of anything else?"

She shook her head. "Once he stopped confiding in me…about anything, I was pretty much in the dark. That's when I paid more attention to his conversations, especially with Palafox." Her voice started to break and she reached under her glasses to wipe the tears from her eyes. "I'm sorry, but I still find it hard to understand why he's doing this to me. We were supposed to be the perfect couple. Soul mates for eternity, he often said." She let out a sigh, and then downed the last of her drink.

Alec looked away for moment. "Listen, if you want to call me sometime or if I can do anything…"

She forced a smile. "I'll be okay. But thanks for offering."

Alec got up slowly. "Can I walk you to your car?"

"You go ahead. I think I'll stay and have another drink"

He pulled out his wallet and dropped a twenty-dollar bill on the table. "Good luck," he said softly.

Alec didn't hear about it until late in the evening when he turned on the TV and caught the end of the eleven o'clock news.

"A woman driving a blue Mazda was killed this afternoon as she left O'Malley's Bar off South Federal Highway in Dania," said the reporter, a young man with a hint of a Boston accent. "According to witnesses on the scene, the woman identified as Patty Leblanc, had pulled into the path of a fast moving pickup which swerved but was unable to avoid slamming into her car."

"Despite efforts by paramedics to save her, the injured woman died moments after arriving at the trauma center at Broward General Medical Center."

"A police officer on the scene was unable to comment as to whether the woman had been drinking. However, at least one person, who had observed her in the bar just moments before, confirmed she had been drinking steadily for over an hour. As is customary in a case like this, the Medical Examiner will determine whether or not alcohol played a part in the accident."

Alec turned off the TV and just sat there. Thoughts of Mrs. Leblanc filled his mind and he wished she'd never called him. If she hadn't, she'd still be alive.

CHAPTER 35

L *ate afternoon*
"I'm looking for a truck to haul my stuff around, fishing gear, camping equipment, that kind of the thing," Alec said to the salesman. They stood underneath a large, unimpressive sign that said: MAJESTIC MOTORS. Bad Credit. No Credit. No Problem.

"Well, you came to the right place," said the salesman, a short skinny guy with a phony smile. He handed Alec his business card. "We just got one a few weeks ago and it might be just what you're interested in." He led the way to a blue truck at the end of a long row of cars.

"Nice looking truck." Alec checked it closely for signs of bodywork and fresh paint. "Twelve grand is a little more than I had in mind."

The salesman smirked. "I can make you a good deal on it, maybe even take a couple hundred off the top. We can finance it too, if you want. Why don't you take it for a spin. If you like it, we can—"

Alec shook his head. "Thanks, but it's not what I'm looking for. Is that the only one you have?"

The salesman hesitated. "Well, there is one other truck. But it's nowhere as good as this one. In fact we use it ourselves to run errands and pick up customers. I'll show it to you if you want."

"Sure. As long as I'm here, why not?"

They went around to the back where a couple of men, one black, the other Latino, were detailing an old Cadillac Seville.

The truck was parked near the office. Alec walked all around it and ran his hand along its sides to check for subtle imperfections. He spotted a couple of telltale smudges above the right rear wheel well. It had recently been painted.

"Was it in a wreck?" He thought about the black truck that had rammed him off the road in the everglades.

"It was a fender bender," the salesman said. "But the frame and engine are in great shape. The marked price is seven thousand nine hundred, but we can knock off five hundred if you're really interested."

Alec crossed his arms. He had to appear that he was just another would-be buyer. "Hmmm. Not a bad deal. Let me think about it. I've got an errand to run but I'll be back by the end of the day." He started to walk off.

"Seven thousand and it's yours," the salesman said, almost shouting.

"Tempting, but I still have to think about it. I'll get back to you."

From inside the office, a tall, gray-bearded man who had been observing them waited until Alec was out of sight, and then came out of the building.

"Who was that?" he said to the salesman. "The way he was checking the truck was almost as if..." He stopped himself. "Do me a favor. Why don't you get his license number?"

"Sure boss." The salesman walked briskly toward the front lot and paused when he saw Alec get into his car. He wrote down the tag number on a small piece of paper and took it back to his boss.

"Thanks," said the boss. He glanced at it quickly, stepped back into the office and dialed a number.

"I thought you'd want to know that some guy was checking out the truck," he said into the phone. "It's probably nothing, but he sure was looking at it strangely. He even ran his hand along the sides, like he was looking for something. Maybe the guy is legit, but then again..."

"Did you get his name?" said a man's voice on the other end.

"No, but we got his tag number." He read it to him slowly.

"Thanks, I'll check it out. In the meantime, don't show the truck to anyone else."

"No problem. I'll put a sold sign across the windshield."

"Good. Call me if he shows up again."

Later, Leblanc called Detective Palafox and repeated what his cousin had said. He gave him the tag number and waited for him to run it through the system.

"It comes back to Santana," Palafox said. "The son-of-a-bitch knows something. But how? You don't suppose—"

"I was thinking the same thing. Patty. She was probably feeding him information. We need to talk."

"I'll be right over."

"Are you trying to avoid me?" Laura said, the second Alec answered the phone. "I called twice, but you didn't return my calls."

"As a matter of fact I was just about to call you." He had her name on a list of messages from the day before.

"Well, the reason I was calling, aside from wanting to know how you're doing, is to let you know I've found a new client for you. She's a lady I met at a gallery. Her name is Jackie Terranova and she's married to this very rich guy who owns a chain of dry cleaners."

"Look, I appreciate what you're doing, but something's come up and, well, you might as well know the truth. I'm back on the case."

"You're kidding. I thought you were putting it behind you to concentrate on your P.I. business. What happened?"

Alec took a moment. "I got a call from Leblanc's wife. She confirmed my suspicions about Palafox. She also told me something about her husband." He sighed. "The trouble is, she died in a car wreck right after our meeting. I had hoped to see her again, after I did some research."

"She died? How awful. What did she say?"

"Enough to convince me that I should follow my instincts. I'm more sure than ever that Palafox and Leblanc were in this together, only now I have no way of proving it. But I'm not giving up, not this time."

"You're really serious about this, aren't you? Well, I'm not going to try to change your mind. But I am going to ask that you take the lady's case. As a favor to me. I already told her you'd take it and I'd hate to disappoint her. I'm supposed to call her to let her know everything's been arranged."

"I'm sorry, Laura, but I really can't do it. Maybe in a few days after—"

"Just talk to her," Laura insisted. "Will you do that for me, at least? If you want, you can refer her to another P.I. or, if she's willing to wait, you can put it off for a week or two."

Alec took a deep breath and exhaled slowly. "All right. Give me her name and phone number."

"You won't regret it." She gave him the information along with what little she knew of the woman's problem. "By the way, she's very attractive, so don't get any ideas."

Alec chuckled. "I'll take it into consideration."

A minute later, he dialed the woman's number and spoke to her briefly. They agreed to meet at his office at ten the next morning.

CHAPTER 36

66 **I** assume Laura told you about my situation," the woman said from across Alec's desk. She looked about forty, blonde and green eyed, with a trace of a southern accent.

"She said you thought your husband was having an affair, but she didn't give any details." He picked up a pen and jotted the woman's name and date on a legal pad. "Why don't you tell me about it?"

The woman started slowly, "Well, a couple of weeks ago, I got a call from a friend, a woman I've known since high school. She said she had seen my husband and a young woman in a restaurant on South Beach. They were laughing and carrying on like a couple of teenagers. At one point, she saw him put his arms around her and…well, I think you get the picture."

Alec nodded. "Is this a divorce matter? If it is, I assume you want the works: photographs, day to day schedule of their meetings, that kind of thing."

She reached into her purse, pulled out a cigarette and waited for Alec to light it. "Actually I'm mostly interested in finding out who she is." She took a quick drag and exhaled to one side. "I probably shouldn't tell you this but before we were married, I was the other woman. So you can understand why I am more than a little concerned. What I'm trying to say is that if my husband is thinking of dumping me for another woman, I want to know about it, so I can prepare myself emotionally as well as financially." She attempted a smile. "A woman has to watch out for herself these days."

Alec put down his pen and crossed his hands over his desk. "I hope you're not in a hurry. I'm working on another case right now."

"As a matter of fact, I am. We're celebrating our seventh anniversary in a couple of weeks and I'd like to know whether or not our marriage is worth celebrating. So, will you do it? Will you take my case?" She took a quick puff on her cigarette, then looked around for an ashtray.

Alec pushed an empty coffee mug toward her and she dropped the cigarette into it. "I'm trying to quit." It sounded like an apology. "I just needed a couple of puffs to satisfy the urge whenever I get angry or nervous, which I am right now. Nervous, that is."

"Two weeks is not a lot of time. I can't promise I'll finish the assignment, at least not with the results you have in mind."

She smiled. "I have confidence in you. Laura said you were the best P.I. in town and that's good enough for me."

Alec smiled back. He ripped off a piece of paper from a legal pad and placed it in front of her. "Why don't you write down everything I should know about your husband. His business address, phone numbers, the kind of car he drives, and his normal schedule. I'll also need a recent photo."

She took a moment to write everything down. When she was finished, she opened a thin leather briefcase and pulled out a photo. "This was taken six months ago. If you need additional information, just let me know."

Alec took a moment to look it over. "Well, I guess that's it. I'll start this afternoon."

"Good. Call me when you find something." She stood up and waited for him to show her to the door.

He'd just returned to his desk when the phone rang. It was Hugo Montenegro, Victor Cardini's uncle, calling from the airport in Miami. "I'm in between flights and thought I'd give you a call to see how things were going," he said, his tone friendly.

"You mean with the investigation? Well, to tell you the truth I've hit a brick wall. As you know, whenever drug money is involved—"

"Drug money?"

"The money that belonged to Victor's father."

"I don't know where you got your information, but the money he was rumored to be hiding did not come from drugs. He was a courier for a counterfeit ring operating between Argentina and Miami."

"You mean the money everyone has been looking for all this time is worthless? I don't know what to say."

"I thought you knew. The fact is, my brother-in-law was scared of drug traffickers and purposely shied away from them and their money."

Alec hesitated. "If what you say is true, then whoever is behind this probably doesn't know the money is bogus."

A loudspeaker blared out a boarding call.

"That's my flight," Hugo said. "I've got to go. Good luck." He hung up and left Alec wondering who else might know the money was counterfeit.

Alec spent the rest of the day checking out the information Mrs. Terranova had provided. With so little to go on, about the only thing he could do was follow Mr. Terranova wherever he went.

For three days straight, he watched the man as he left for work, went out to lunch or an appointment, and returned home at the end of the day. On the fourth day, which was Friday, Mr. Terranova left for work as usual. But instead of driving to his office on Biscayne Boulevard, he drove to an apartment building near the airport. He parked his car, got out and walked up two flights of stairs visible from the street.

From his car parked nearby, Alec watched as Mr. Terranova knocked on the third door from the stairs. He carried a brightly covered package under his arm. Soon, the door opened and he disappeared into the apartment.

Twenty minutes later, Mr. Terranova emerged from the apartment and walked back down the stairs. He smiled as he got into his car and drove away.

Alec waited a couple of minutes, then got out and walked up the stairs. He knocked on the same door.

A young woman opened the door. "Did you forget something?" She looked to be in her early twenties, thin build, not too tall and wore her long, auburn hair in a ponytail. "Oh, I thought you were somebody else."

Alec smiled. "I'm looking for Cynthia Chavez. Does she live here?"

She shook her head. "Maybe she was the lady who had the apartment before me. You may want to try the manager. He's in apartment 1A, downstairs."

"Thanks, I think I'll do that." He turned around and walked down the stairs. He stopped briefly to look at the directory above the mailboxes and took note of the name, Jennifer Perry, apartment 3F.

He couldn't wait to get back to his office to check out her name.

CHAPTER 37

Leblanc frowned as he read a note that someone had slipped in his mailbox. It said: *I know what you did and you can't get away with it.*

He crumpled it in his hand and went back inside and dialed a number.

"He's on to us," he said, the second Palafox answered the phone. "He left me a note." His voice wobbled. "What are we going to do?"

"The son-of-a-bitch is bluffing, 'cause he doesn't know shit. He's just trying to scare you."

"Well, he's doing a good job. I don't know how much more of this I can take. When is it going to be over, I mean really over?"

Palafox sighed. "Look, I know how you feel, but you have to hang in there. Give me a few days and I'll guarantee Santana will no longer be a problem."

"What about the money?" Leblanc asked, but Palafox had already hung up.

It didn't take long for Alec to run a check on Jennifer Perry. There were no big surprises, except that today was her birthday. She'd just turned twenty-three, which would explain the package Mr. Terranova was carrying.

Alec went over her information, waited a moment, and then dialed Mrs. Terranova's number. No answer. He left a message for her to call, which she did ten minutes later.

"So, who is she?" Mrs. Terranova said eagerly.

"Her name is Jennifer Perry and she lives in an apartment near the airport. After three days of tailing your husband wherever he went, I finally got lucky. This morning, after he left for work, I followed him to her apartment."

"Bastard," she said, under her breath.

"By the way, today's her birthday. She just turned twenty-three. I'll put the complete report in an envelope. You can pick it up at my office or I can mail it to you, however you want."

"Can you fax it to me? I want to have it in my hands when I confront my husband this evening."

"You sure you want to do that. If I were you I'd think about it and wait a day or two, maybe longer."

"Thanks for the advice, but I want it over, the sooner the better. I'll be waiting for your fax."

Alec hesitated. "Can you do me a favor? Can you give me an extra day to check something out?"

"Check what out?"

"When I met Jennifer under a pretext, I was a little surprised. She wasn't what I expected. She was kind of homely and her body...well, let's just say you've got her beat in that department."

"Are you trying to say she's not the one my husband is seeing?"

"No, that's not what I mean." He paused. "Look, can you humor me on this? Just give me until noon tomorrow."

"Well, all right. I guess another day won't make a difference."

Alec's plan was simple: call Mr. Terranova, catch him off guard, ask him a question about Jennifer.

He made the call a little after nine the next morning. "My name is Bob Thompson from Speedway Motors," Alec said, speaking rapidly. "I'm calling to verify a credit application from Miss Jennifer Perry. On the application she listed you as a co-signer, which means we'll need your signature as well. She indicates that you're her father, is that correct?"

"No. I mean yes," Mr. Terranova said. "Maybe I should speak to Jennifer before we go any further."

"Yes, I suggest you do. Thank you for your time. Have a nice day."

Alec pressed the Off button, waited a couple of seconds, and then dialed Mrs. Terranova's number.

"You have nothing to worry about." Alec grinned. "Your husband isn't having an affair."

"Well, then who is she? Why is he seeing her behind my back?"

"Are you ready for this? Jennifer is his daughter. What tipped me off were her features. She looked like your husband: the contour of her mouth, her nose, and especially her eyes."

"But my husband has no daughters, at least not from his previous marriage. How did you find this out?"

"It was easy. I called him, under pretext, and I got him to admit she was his daughter. My guess is that he found out about her only recently and he didn't tell you because he didn't know how you'd react."

"I don't know what to say." She started to cry. "I was expecting the worst and now… How can I thank you?"

"You just did. Happy anniversary."

CHAPTER 38

"I'm so glad you were able to make it," Julie said, from across the dining room table. "We should do this more often."

"I agree. You and Ben always made feel like family. It's nice to know that our friendship will continue." He poured some more wine into her glass.

"There's an extra chop on the stove. I can get it for you if you're still hungry."

Alec hesitated. "Sure, why not? It's not every day I get to eat a real home-cooked meal."

Julie laughed. "Well, it's your fault, you know. There are plenty of women out there who would make a good wife for you, if you'd only give them a chance." She got up and stepped into the kitchen.

"I tried that, remember? Sometimes I think guys like me are meant to be bachelors forever." He grinned. "Then again if the right girl should come along…"

The phone rang and Julie picked up the extension. "Yes." She nodded. "He's right here." She walked back to the dining room. "It's for you." She cupped a hand over the mouthpiece. "I could barely understand him."

"For me? That's strange. I didn't tell anyone I'd be here." He took the phone. "Hello?"

"The next time you leave a note at somebody's house they may think you're trying to rob them and you could wind up being on the six o'clock news," said a man with a muffled voice.

"What the fuck are you talking about?" Alec got up and moved to the other side of the room.

"Don't play dumb. You think you know something, don't you? Well, you don't know shit, so leave it alone. By the way, your girlfriend, Laura, sure looks good in pink, standing in front of the window, getting ready to go to bed. It's enough to give some sicko a reason to go in there and do all sorts of things to her. Am I getting through?"

"Look, asshole, if I catch you anywhere near her, I'll—"

The caller hung up.

Alec stood there and shook his head, then walked back to the table and set the phone down.

"What was that about?" Julie asked.

Alec shook his head. "I'd like to tell you what's going on but I can't. The less you know the better."

"This is about Ben's case and the missing money, isn't it?"

"I'm sorry, but I have to go." He turned toward the door. "I promise that when this is all over, I'll tell you all about it."

Julie sighed. "You're a great guy, Alec. I'd hate for something to happen to you. Whatever it is that you're doing, please be careful."

He forced a smile. "I will." He kissed her on the cheek and quickly left the house.

On the road, Alec called Laura's number and got her answering machine. "Laura, this is Alec. Pick up the phone, it's important. Do you hear me? Pick it up." Short pause. "I'm on the way to your house."

He didn't hear from her and got there thirty-five minutes later.

"Laura, it's Alec." He banged on the door. "Are you okay?" A moment later, he heard footsteps and the sound of a deadbolt unlocking.

"What's all the racket about?" Laura, said, opening the door. "What are you doing here?" She wore a pink satin robe.

"Is everything all right?" Alec walked in. "I tried calling but you didn't answer."

She closed the door behind him. "I was in my studio reading and listening to music. Wagner tends to get a little loud at times, so I probably didn't hear the phone ring."

"Jesus, a guy could come in here and rob you blind and you probably wouldn't even know it."

She ran her hands through her hair and took a seat on the couch. "You still haven't told me what you're doing here." She sounded annoyed.

"Give me a second." Alec walked across the room and looked out into the street, then ambled back to the couch. "Somebody was watching you just a few minutes ago as you stood by the window. He called me while I was at Julie Brody's place, to let me know what you were wearing. He was trying to send me a message—get off the case or else."

"Or else what?"

"He knows where you live, what time you go to bed," he said, exasperated. "Do I have to draw you a picture?"

"You're scaring me, Alec. Maybe you should do as he says and just drop it."

Alec took a deep breath "I'm afraid it's too late and he knows it. That's why he's trying to get to me any way he can." He shook his head. "I'm really sorry about it. I didn't think he'd bring you into this."

"Who do you think it was?"

"The voice was muffled, but if I had to guess, I'd say it was either Leblanc or his buddy Palafox." He looked around the room. "If it'll make you feel safer, I can stick around, maybe even spend the night."

Laura thought about it for a moment. "I'll be all right, but thanks for offering. I'll keep my phone handy and believe me, you'll be the first person I call if I see anyone lurking around."

He nodded. "Well, I know it's late and you probably want to go to bed."

"I am a little tired." She stood up. "By the way, Jackie Terranova called and told about the great job you did for her. I'd say this calls for a celebration."

Alec smiled. "Sure, only this time I'll pick the time and place."

"Fine with me." She reached up and put her lips to his, holding her breath for a long moment.

She smiled. "That's just so you won't forget."

CHAPTER 39

By week's end, Alec had run out of leads. He was no closer to making a connection between Leblanc and Palafox and the missing money. Frustrated, he decided to pay Leblanc a visit.

When he rang the bell just before noon, a petite, Asian-looking woman wearing a yellow jump suit, opened the door.

"My name is Alec Santana. Is Ray home? I was in the neighborhood, so I thought I'd stop and say hello. We're old friends." He flashed a smile.

"Then you must be a former cop. It seems that all his friends are ex-cops. Please come in." She opened the door wider to let him in. "He's in the back doing some yard work. I'll let him know you're here."

A moment later, Leblanc appeared, his thin, unshaven face looking hot and sweaty. They exchanged pleasantries and stepped into the kitchen.

"I hope you don't mind me dropping in like this," Alec said, "but I need to ask you a couple of questions. It'll only take a moment."

Leblanc poured himself a glass of water and took a big gulp. "Like I told you before, it's been too many years. I basically put the case out of my mind. "Did you ever find her...the girl with the Spanish name?" He pulled out a chair and sat down at the breakfast table.

Alec sat down across from him and folded his arms. "Rosario turned out to be a city in Argentina. But you already knew that, didn't you?"

"What are you talking about?" Leblanc said, his hand still wrapped around the glass.

"Just before he was killed, Johnson laid it all out for me. The trouble is, I'm not sure who's behind it, though I have my suspicions."

"You're talking in riddles. What is it you want to ask me?"

"Tell me about Palafox."

"What do you mean?"

"He's the one who's calling the shots. Right? When this thing breaks wide open, which I know it will, I sure wouldn't want to be in your shoes."

Leblanc took a long drink from his glass and set it down slowly. "I have no idea what you're talking about. If this is what you came to tell me, you're wasting your time."

"Maybe." Alec shrugged. "But just so you know, I'm not giving up. So you can tell your buddy Palafox that I don't scare easily and he can stop with the phone calls. I knew it was him the moment he mentioned Laura."

Leblanc's jaw muscles twitched and he took another drink. "I think you'd better leave," he said tersely. His muscles were still twitching as he got up and escorted Alec to the door.

"One last thing," Alec said before Leblanc closed the door. "I assume you know about the money. If you don't, you're in for a big surprise." He smiled when he saw a puzzled look on Leblanc's face.

"You sure nobody followed you?" Palafox said. They sat at a picnic table in the middle of a small park just off 135th Street.

A homeless man wearing a wrinkled brown jacket stood next to an open trashcan on the other side of the park. He stared at them for a moment before digging into the trash.

"Nobody followed me, all right," Leblanc said, annoyed at the question. "Now listen to me. We gotta do something and we gotta do it fast. Santana came to my house an hour ago. My girlfriend let him in, thinking he and I were buddies."

"I don't fucking believe it." Palafox shook his head. "You didn't talk to him, did you?"

"I had to. What else could I do? But don't worry, I didn't tell him anything. I let him do all the talking. The thing is, he seemed to know everything, even mentioned you. But of course I played dumb. Finally, I put an end to it, and told him to leave."

"What exactly did he say?"

"Not much. He thinks you're calling the shots—he wanted me to confirm it."

"Look, maybe he doesn't know everything, but he knows enough to put us in jail. I think it's time to put an end to this once and for all."

They paused when the homeless man walked toward them. They tried to ignore him, but he kept on coming. When he was less than ten feet away, he stopped and held out his hand.

"Can you spare some change?" He had a gaunt, ghostly look and smelled as though he hadn't bathed in a long time.

"Beat it," Leblanc said. "Go bother somebody else."

The man didn't move. "Please Mister, I'm hungry. I haven't had a decent meal in days. All I need is a couple of quarters."

Palafox made sure no one was watching, then reached for his gun and pointed it at the homeless man's head. "Get the hell away from here or I swear I'll blow your fucking head off," he shouted. "Do you understand?"

The man's eyes lit up and he turned and quickly walked away.

Palafox put the gun back in its holster. "If I knew I could get away with it, I would've shot the bastard, just to do the world a favor." He waited a second. "As I was about to say, I think Santana was pushing your buttons to see how you'd react. It's an old trick. You should've known that, for Christ's sake. So, what else did he have to say?"

"Right before I closed the door on him he asked if I knew about the money, and if I didn't, I was in for a big surprise."

Palafox thought about it for a moment. "It doesn't make sense. Not that it matters, 'cause he's the one who's in for a big surprise." He glanced around. "Let's get out of here. We've been sitting here too long. Why don't we meet tonight at the Chinese restaurant near Laurenzo's market and I'll tell you what I think we should do."

Leblanc nodded. "I'll see you there about eight."

CHAPTER 40

The phone rang just before midnight. Half awake, Alec reached over to answer it.

"Alec, listen to me," Laura whispered. "I've been kidnapped. Palafox and Leblanc are convinced I know where the money is, which is crazy. They think Jeff told me all about it."

It took a second for the words to sink in. "Where are you? Give me a location, a landmark, anything that stands out."

"I'm being held in a house in the woods somewhere near Stuart." She rushed her words. "On a road called Spanish...Spanish something, just west of the turnpike. There's a large wrought iron gate with the letter M at the top and—"

"Get off the phone, you fucking bitch. Put it down," said a man's voice in the background.

The line went dead.

Stuart was an easy two-hour drive, straight up the turnpike. When Alec saw the exit sign up ahead, he slowed, put on his blinkers and got off. He stopped at the nearest gas station to ask for directions.

"Excuse me," he said to a man filling a black Hummer. "Do you happen to know of a street around here: Spanish something or other?"

The man nodded. "Spanish Trace. It's about two and a half miles, just off Martin Highway." He pointed west toward Indiantown. "Look for a small church with a bell on top; the street is just beyond it."

"Thanks." Alec drove off and got back on the road.

Minutes later he spotted the small church and turned left on Spanish Trace. He drove slowly looking for the house like the one Laura had described. When he got to the end of the street, he shook his head. Maybe it was on the other side of the highway. He turned around.

He had just crossed Martin Highway when he spotted the letter M on a gate in front of a house set back in the woods. He parked on the side of the road, got out and ran toward the back. The place was dark except for a room with a large window facing an open patio. He glanced around, and then made a quick dash toward the house. When he peered through the window, he saw Palafox standing over Laura. She sat on a chair in the middle of the room, her hands tied behind her back.

"I'm telling you the truth." She cried and shook her head. "I don't know where the money is. If I did, I would give it to you. Why can't you believe me?"

Palafox took a step backward and folded his arms. "I'll make a deal with you. You tell me where the money is and we'll split it fifty-fifty. It's a one-time offer. If you refuse, there's no telling what my friend Leblanc might want to do with you when he gets back. The guy's a fucking psycho. I'd rather tangle with a hungry alligator than deal with him when he's mad, which he's going to be if you don't tell me where the money is. Am I getting through?"

"For the last time, I don't know where the money is," she said, her voice rising. "The truth is, Jeff and I had a crappy marriage and I was planning to divorce him before he killed himself. He had no reason to tell me where it was or what he planned to do with it."

Palafox's face turned red and he slapped her across the cheek. Blood trickled out of her mouth. "I'm tired of this shit." He pulled out a switchblade and held it up to her face, and then to her neck. "Tell me where it is! Tell me, or I'll cut you. I swear I'll do it, if you don't tell me this very second."

Alec took a couple of deep breaths, then grabbed a heavy metal chair and smashed it against the window. The glass shattered in all directions.

"Drop it!" He leaped into the room. He pointed his gun at Palafox.

Startled, Palafox stepped back and threw down the knife.

"Now untie her."

Palafox hesitated. "I don't think so," he said with a smirk.

"Put the gun down or I'll blow your fucking head off," said a voice from behind.

Alec froze, and then dropped the gun on the floor. At the same time, Leblanc came around, picked up the gun and handed it to Palafox. "You couldn't leave it alone, could you? Well, too bad 'cause your luck just ran out."

Palafox waited a moment, then walked behind Laura and untied her.

"Let's get this over with." She stood up, stretching her limbs.

"Wh-what's going on?" Alec's eyes moved between Laura and the two men.

Palafox stepped forward and aimed his gun at Alec's head. "I'll tell you what's going. Your girlfriend here set you up. You should've backed off when you had the chance."

"You won't get away with this," Alec said. "I'm not the only one who knows what the two of you were doing. Besides, it's all been for nothing. The money is bogus."

"What the fuck are you talking about?" Palafox said.

"I'm telling you that the money they found fifteen years ago was counterfeit. The guy that died in the fire was a courier for a ring from Argentina. His brother-in-law told me all about it."

"He's lying," Leblanc said. "Just shoot the bastard so we can get the hell out of here."

"There's one way to find out," Alec said. "Just look at one of the bills under the light and you'll see some minor imperfections."

"He's stalling," Leblanc said.

"Maybe," Palafox said. He turned to Laura. "What about it? You've seen the money. Does it look real?"

"It looked real to me," she said. "You can see for yourself once you've kept your end of the bargain by putting a bullet in his head."

"I told you he was lying," Leblanc shouted. "Are you going to shoot him or not?"

"Wait," Laura said. "Let me do it. I want to see what it feels like." She grabbed the gun from Palafox and pressed it against Alec's head. "Sorry Alec. Nothing personal. I hope you understand."

In an instant she moved the muzzle to the left and shot Palafox and then Leblanc who looked truly shocked as he dropped to the floor. He moaned as she walked over and shot him in the head, and then kicked his gun to the side.

Stunned, Alec just stood there. "Why didn't you kill me?" he said, perspiration building over his eyebrows.

"I don't know. Maybe because I like you and I thought we could take the money and start a new life together." She half smiled. "It's a pretty good offer, I'd say. The question is, can I trust you to make the right decision?"

"I'm beginning to understand. You used them and they thought they were using you. It was very clever of you to leave the note in Leblanc's mail box, to make him think I had done it."

"I had to make them believe you knew more than you did, that they had to act quickly, which they did by setting a trap for you. Our deal was that once you were out of the way, we would split the money three ways. But I changed my mind."

"You're wealthy, why would you need—"

"It was all a front. My previous husband left me with a big house on the water and some money, which wasn't nearly enough to allow me to live the way I had gotten used to. Jeff knew I had run out of money and a few months ago when I was threatening to leave him, he told me about the hidden money. He offered to dig into it and give me as much as I wanted. Naturally I played along, at least until he showed me where he had stashed it. He told me all about the agreement he and the others had made about splitting it."

Alec listened and kept an eye on the gun.

"But there was only one problem. The other cops were expecting their share. That's when I approached Leblanc, who I knew had a shady past, to help me come up with a plan to get rid of them, one by one. He's the one who brought in Palafox. Everything was working fine until you started playing detective, which meant you had to be killed as well."

"What about Jeff? I assume his death wasn't a suicide."

She sighed. "Poor, pathetic Jeff. We had no choice but to get rid of him. Just so you know, I did love him, but that was a long time ago before he gained thirty pounds and turned into an alcoholic."

A long pause, and then Alec said, "About the money. It isn't going to do you any good. You know that, don't you? It's worthless except what you can get from a con artist who's willing to take it off your hands."

"You're not serious, are you? I thought you were saying it just to buy time. Damn it, Alec, tell me the truth."

"When they found the money, everyone assumed it came from a drug deal, which is usually the case when money is found hidden like that, inside a wall or some other place. Victor's father belonged to a counterfeit ring but they had no way of knowing it at the time."

Laura relaxed her hand holding the gun. "So what are we supposed to do? The money's got to be worth something, right? How much? How much can we get if we unload it?"

Alec shook his head. "It's hard to say and it won't be that easy, assuming you can find someone with the right connections."

Palafox had taken two shots to the torso. Blood oozed out of his wounds. Barely conscious, he kept still while his hand slowly made its way to a gun from an ankle holster. He grabbed it and aimed at Laura.

"Behind you!" Alec shouted.

The gun fired just as she spun around.

Palafox let out a gasp and released his hold on the gun. Alec rushed over to make sure he was dead, and then turned to Laura who'd caught a round in her chest. She breathed hard as she went into shock.

"I'll call an ambulance." He started to dial and paused. Images of his friend, Ben Brody, and the Johnsons flashed through his mind.

"Help me. Don't let me die. Please, Alec, don't let me die."

He hung up the phone and calmly walked away. Halfway to the door he stopped in his tracks. He couldn't do it. As much as he wanted to, he couldn't just leave her there. Slowly, he turned back around.

He learned the next day that she died on the way to the hospital, and for a second he almost felt sad. Then he felt nothing as he stared at her portrait hanging on his bedroom wall. He really did like the older face, he thought as he took it down and placed it next to the outgoing trash.

DON'T MISS ERNESTO PATINO'S OTHER NOVELS:

WEB OF SECRETS

A phone call from a blackmailer turned Sarah Baker's life upside down. The man claimed to know the circumstances of her illegal adoption thirty years ago. He also revealed some shocking facts about her real parents.

Hiring a Private Investigator seemed the only option, but it meant opening a Pandora's box. Sarah needed confirmation and closure, and was willing to take the risk. Ex-FBI investigator turned P.I. Joe Coopersmith was up for the task, but working on a thirty-year-old mystery wouldn't be easy. Joe didn't realize it might also turn deadly…

IN THE SHADOW OF A STRANGER

2014 Indie Excellence Book Award Finalist—Thriller category

As a result of a chance encounter with a Holocaust survivor on vacation in Mexico City, young attorney Antonio de la Vega learns that his natural father is a former SS officer who committed heinous crimes against the Jews during World War II. Obsessed with the idea of meeting his father, Antonio embarks on a search that takes him from Mexico to the United States and ultimately to South America, meeting ageing ex-Nazis, vengeful Jews, and an alluring young woman who has been assigned to watch his every move.

ONE LAST DANCE—Coming Soon

For those who believe that fate and destiny play a role in our lives. Two young people come together, fall in love and bring new meaning to the phase Que Sera, Sera. What will be, will be. The novel is set in the world of ballroom dancing.

About Author Ernesto Patino

Ernesto Patino is a former FBI agent. He lives in Southern Arizona where he divides his time between writing and working as a private investigator.

Visit Ernesto's website: www.ernestopatino.com

www.ingramcontent.com/pod-product-compliance
Lightning Source LLC
Chambersburg PA
CBHW071244130626
46556CB00003B/1160